FIRST CONTACT

Talia trailed behind Ladan ... her head crowded with strange, conflicting emotions over which she had no control. She'd been frightened when she left the valley's shelter, but then she looked up and saw Ladan's towering form. Somehow, she knew, she'd be safe with him, that he would guard and protect her.

When the sandstorm hit, her belief had only been strengthened. If she had not been in Ladan's arms, she would have bolted, running madly from the noise and terror.

The rightness of being in his arms puzzled her. She'd been taught proper respect for another being was shown by not touching ... but touching seemed pleasant. When she woke to find Ladan softly caressing her palm, the pleasure was exquisite. When he placed his lips on her skin, her heart leapt from her chest.

As she walked through the cold night, she tried to block his presence from her mind but found it impossible to erect a barrier against him. It was as if there was a homing device in him, and she carried the receptor. Now that the Dark Hunter had entered her life, nothing would ever be the same. He was her destiny ...

YOU WON'T WANT TO READ JUST ONE—KATHERINE STONE

ROOMMATES (0-8217-5206-5, $6.99/$7.99)
No one could have prepared Carrie for the monumental changes she would face when she met her new circle of friends at Stanford University. Once their lives intertwined and became woven into the tapestry of the times, they would never be the same.

TWINS (0-8217-5207-3, $6.99/$7.99)
Brook and Melanie Chandler were so different, it was hard to believe they were sisters. One was a dark, serious, ambitious New York attorney; the other, a golden, glamourous, sophisticated supermodel. But they were more than sisters—they were twins and more alike than even they knew . . .

THE CARLTON CLUB (0-8217-5204-9, $6.99/$7.99)
It was the place to see and be seen, the only place to be. And for those who frequented the playground of the very rich, it was a way of life. Mark, Kathleen, Leslie and Janet—they worked together, played together, and loved together, all behind exclusive gates of the *Carlton Club*.

Available wherever paperbacks are sold, or order direct from the Publisher. Send cover price plus 50¢ per copy for mailing and handling to Penguin USA, P.O. Box 999, c/o Dept. 17109, Bergenfield, NJ 07621. Residents of New York and Tennessee must include sales tax. DO NOT SEND CASH.

HUNTER'S HEART

Leann Harris

Pinnacle Books
Kensington Publishing Corp.

http://www.pinnaclebooks.com

PINNACLE BOOKS are published by

Kensington Publishing Corp.
850 Third Avenue
New York, NY 10022

Copyright © 1997 by Barbara Harrison

All rights reserved. No part of this book may be reproduced in any form or by any means without the prior written consent of the Publisher, excepting brief quotes used in reviews.

If you purchased this book without a cover, you should be aware that this book is stolen property. It was reported as "unsold and destroyed" to the Publisher and neither the Author nor the Publisher has received any payment for this "stripped book."

Pinnacle and the P logo Reg. U.S. Pat. & TM Off.

First Printing: May, 1997
10 9 8 7 6 5 4 3 2 1

Printed in the United States of America

To Dr. Herman Harrison for all your help and input. Whoever thought when I typed your dissertation all those years ago, sweetheart, that I would learn so much.

Chapter 1

Ladan fingered the glass of cheap liquor before him. He hadn't asked the bartender the name of the drink. All he'd wanted was something strong so he would look like he belonged. That's what he got.

He glanced around the crowded, noisy bar. The smell of unwashed bodies assailed his nose. Obviously, bathing wasn't a high priority in this world. But what could one expect on a mining planet like Petar?

The patrons had been mighty closed-mouthed when he questioned them earlier. No one knew anything about anything, and certainly no one had heard about the old man.

Slowly, he surveyed the room. In the corner, a shriveled up woman of undetermined age made eye contact with him. She nodded toward the door, stood, and left.

Realizing that this could be a trap, as the officials of this world would like nothing better than for him to meet his end on their dusty part of the star system,

Ladan followed her out of the bar and carefully surveyed the street. Nothing seemed out of place. No menace.

The woman disappeared into a shop four doors down, a combination general store, pharmacy, and tattoo parlor. He waited until a light appeared in the window before entering.

She motioned for him to join her on a tall stool behind the counter. Her eyes narrowed as she studied him from the top of his head to the tips of his black boots. Her gaze traveled back to the studded, black leather half-gloves that covered his hands.

"Who are you?" she asked. A hint of fear tinged her voice.

"My name is Ladan."

Her little gasp told him she recognized his name. "The bounty hunter." She shook her head. "I should've guessed." She climbed down from the stool and moved around the counter.

His harsh reputation must have scared her. He needed to reassure her that he would not harm the old man he sought. "If you know my name, then you know that I would never work for the Dyne."

She stopped and looked over her shoulder. "You are also known as the Omus Teeha—the deadly one." The statement sounded like an accusation. "Others call you Dark Hunter, for it is said no one you have hunted escapes capture."

"That's true. It's also true I have only one tenet ruling my life, and that is to defeat the Dyne."

"Why do you seek this man?"

"He is the only person who can reactivate the defense shields and save the Kanta Alliance."

The woman hesitated.

"Do you want the Alliance to win? Or would you rather live again under the Dyne's harsh rule?"

Her eyes darkened and Ladan picked up on her fear. He didn't doubt that she recalled the time before the Kanta Alliance. It was a bloody, dark history that no one wanted to relive.

"You remember what it was like when the Dyne were masters of the worlds, don't you, old woman?"

She nodded. "I've heard rumors about the old man who lives in the mountains beyond the desert. I cannot say if they are true. All I know is what I have overheard from the mountain traders. You must judge for yourself."

He stood and placed several gold coins on the counter. "My thanks."

The old woman scooped up the coins and put them in her pocket. "Good luck, Dark Hunter."

He paused by the door. "Luck, I've found, is fickle. I rely only on skill."

Heat rose in shimmering waves from white sand. Ladan squinted against the glare as he looked to the purple mountains in the distance, his final destination.

He cursed the day and a half it had taken him on this miserable planet to discover where the Geala lived. Every hour he was delayed meant that the Alliance was that much weaker. The moment he learned the Geala's location, he tried to rent a vehicle to take him through the desert, but none were available. All the vehicles in town belonged to Dalfex, the mining company that owned and ruled the planet. Ladan had crossed lasers with the officials of the corporation on more than one occasion, and no one at Dalfex would give him spit on a hot day, let alone loan him a vehicle. But if they thought their refusal would stop him, they were sadly mistaken. He'd left the ugly little town and started across the desert on foot.

The heat scorching the sands didn't bother him. He came from a desolate planet, where the fight for life was won only by the fittest, toughest men who could bend the land and elements to their will.

Some said his people had evolved from lizards, because of their unique golden eyes with diamond-shaped pupils, scaly skin, and brutal strength. Ladan knew differently. The harsh scaling of skin across his forehead and back of the hands was nature's way of protecting him from the raging sandstorms that plagued his home.

Ladan hated the betraying traits of his heritage as much as he hated the man who sired him, so he encased both his hands in half-gloves and allowed his hair to fall over his forehead, holding it down with a thong.

Ladan felt a pull from the distant peaks. All was not right. He began to run, his long powerful legs eating up the sand. When he reached the foot of the mountains, unwinded, he began his ascent.

The sudden scream of Dyne fighter planes shattered the stillness. Now he knew the reason for the urgency he felt. His enemy was hunting the same prey.

Like a beacon, the black cloud of rising smoke led him into a lush, broad valley. Cultivated fields took up one end, while at the other stood the remains of a large stone dwelling.

He scanned the length of the valley and surrounding mountains, searching for any further sign of the Dyne. When he found none, he threaded his way through the fields, moving toward the house. The unnatural quiet set his nerves humming. Without a sound, he slipped into the smoldering building. He stilled and listened for any sign of life.

"Father." The soft, melodic voice floated down the wooden stairs. The sound drew him up steps to the second story. He stopped as soon as he could see into the room. Kneeling a few feet from the top step was a lone female. It appeared she held someone's hand who was buried in the rubble.

He could not see the woman's face, but glorious golden hair spilled over her shoulders, down her back and onto the floor. When she moved, he caught a glimpse of lavender material under the thick mane.

Suddenly, the girl went still. He knew he had not made a sound, but somehow she must have sensed his presence. Before he could move, she grabbed the laser gun lying by her left side, turned and fired. Ladan ignored the burning pain in his arm as he leaped through the air and tackled her. His powerful fingers encircled her slender wrist, squeezing until she dropped the weapon.

A bolt of awareness sizzled through him as his fingertips came into contact with the girl's smooth skin.

Soft.

She was so incredibly soft, like nothing he had ever touched before.

He glanced at both her hands. Much to his surprise, she held no weapon. Instead, he noticed the mark in the female's open left palm. In the center of her hand was a network of veins that resembled a six-point star—the mark of the Geala.

The warmest, most sensitive part of their body, the blue star, had become the death sentence to the Geala.

No matter how they disguised themselves, the star gave them away to the Dyne's hired assassins.

His eyes flew to her face, expecting the pale coloring of the Geala, but instead, he found indigo blue eyes surrounded by thick, golden lashes. Her palm declared her Geala, but her golden hair and peach-tinted skin said her blood was mixed—like his.

Fear and panic clouded her beautiful eyes, and for some reason he didn't comprehend, Ladan sought to reassure her. "Joakim, the First Secretary of the Alliance, sent me."

Her face showed no reaction, no dawning knowledge.

"Let me see the ring," a man's reedy voice rasped.

Ladan jumped at the sound. He had forgotten the man pinned beneath a large wooden beam until this moment. Startled, he released the girl and stood. The old one had to be Toaeth, the one he sought.

From the inside pocket of his vest, Ladan withdrew the ring and handed it to him. As Toaeth inspected the ring, Ladan tried to move the wooden beam lying across the old man's chest, but it would not yield to his strength.

"Do not waste your time trying to free me. I'm dying." Toaeth coughed. "Why have you come?"

Ladan squatted by the man's head. "The Alliance has been weakened by the continual raids of the Dyne and they need you to reactivate the computer. But—" Ladan glanced around the destruction. "It seems I'm too late. The Dyne have won."

Toaeth smiled weakly. "No, they have not. Talia, my daughter, knows the secret. Take her."

The girl moved to her father's side. She reached out to brush back the silver strands from his bloodied brow, then drew her hand back. "What secret, Father? I know no secret."

"Trust me, Talia, you carry the knowledge within, and when you are called to act, you will know the way . . ." The last word trailed off. With a final wheezing breath, Toaeth died.

Ladan watched as the girl threw back her head and battled to subdue the anguish he knew was in her heart. The Geala frowned on any outward show of emotion. In spite of her efforts, one lone tear slipped down her cheek. Mixed blood would always tell, as he had been so brutally reminded all his life.

With poise and elegance, Talia rose. "I will help you free him, then prepare him for burial." She looked down at her father.

He grasped her by the arms. Her startled gaze flew to his face. "No, we cannot bury him. The Dyne will be here soon to confirm the kill."

Her eyes widened in horror.

"Listen to me, Talia. Right now the most important thing is to get you safely to Ezion Geber. Millions of people are depending on you to save them."

The heavy pain in her heart was clearly reflected in her expression. "But to leave him . . ."

Uncomfortable with the feelings she stirred in him, he shook her. "Those assassins are going to want a body. I'm going to give it to them, and pray they are satisfied they killed the last living Geala." He released her and stepped away. "Go, pack a change of clothes and a cloak. Nights on the desert are cold."

"We cannot travel through the mountains in the dark. I do not know the way. I have never been outside the valley."

Ladan cursed. Nothing, it seemed, was going to be

easy on this quest. "I know the way, but the trail was so steep and winding I don't want to risk it in the dark. I'll find a place for us to hide, but we can't stay close to this house."

He saw her slender frame tremble, but she fought the fear by raising her chin and taking a deep breath. "I do not know your name. What is it?"

If she was to travel half the galaxy with him, she had the right to know his name. "Ladan. My name is Ladan."

"Thank you." She disappeared into the undamaged portion of the house.

He had to give her credit. The little half-breed had courage. He hoped she had enough to carry her through the hell of the next few days.

Ladan heard the crunch of the boots as someone picked a path through the debris. He drew his laser and melted into the shadows and waited.

"Ladan, I have packed some food—"

Talia's voice caused the intruder to whirl and in the moonlight Ladan could see an old-fashioned gun in his hand. Ladan fired. The stranger screamed and dropped the pistol. Several more men swarmed forward, their weapons drawn.

"Stop, stop," Talia cried, rushing between Ladan and the other men. "Do not do this."

"Get away from them, Talia," Ladan ordered.

She whirled. "They are friends."

Ladan studied the men. They were small—a full head shorter than Ladan's own 6'2"—dressed in padded coats, fur hats, and brightly colored pants. Each man held a rifle aimed directly at Ladan's chest. The weapons were old, but well cared for, and a person was just as dead from one of their bullets as a blast from a laser gun.

"We saw the smoke as we were crossing the desert," the wounded man said, "and came to see if you were all right. Are you, Lady Talia?" The man looked pointedly at Ladan as he asked the question.

"Father was killed, Dee."

"Did he do it?" Dee asked, pointing to Ladan.

"No." Talia glanced around the circle of men. "Please, my friends, put down your weapons. Ladan came to take Father with him to help . . ."

"The Alliance," Ladan supplied when it became obvious she had forgotten the name.

"Yes, that was it. Now that Father is dead, I am to go with Ladan."

At the sound of his name, a rumble ran through the group. Dee stepped forward. "Do you know who this man is, my lady? He is also known as the Dark Hunter," Dee spat out. "He is the most brutal bounty hunter in the star system. More than once he has brought back his prey dead. He is feared by all."

Ladan's eyes burned with rage. "The female will be of no use to the Alliance dead." Out of the corner of his eye, Ladan saw Talia freeze.

Hell he mumbled to himself. He was frightening the girl, who he'd bet had never experienced anything like the vibrating hostility between him and Dee.

"We don't have time for this," Ladan growled. "The danger hasn't passed. The Dyne will come to confirm their kill. Talia and I need to get away from here."

Dee grunted something under his breath, then said, "While you are gone, we'll bury your father and repair the damage to your home."

"No." The word exploded from Ladan's lips. "Nothing must be touched. The assassins must believe they have been successful in their kill. The female's life depends on it."

Dee looked like he wanted to argue. Instead, he turned to his men and whispered a command. They withdrew. "Good luck, Talia. We'll await your return." Without another word, he disappeared into the night.

Although they did not look at each other, Ladan and Talia were aware of every movement the other made.

"Are you ready?" Ladan asked.

"Yes." There was an odd catch in her voice, but he refused to look at her. He didn't want to see her pain.

Ladan located a cave at the top of the pass leading out of the valley. With the moonlight washing the landscape, he could see the entire valley. If the Dyne came, he would know.

As he watched for the enemy, the suspicion floating in the back of his mind surfaced. Someone had betrayed him to the Dyne. That was the only logical explanation for their knowing he was in this section of the star system, let alone the fighters finding the valley minutes before him. And someone on this planet had been bribed, because the defensive shields around this planet had been lowered to allow the Dyne free fight over the surface.

"What are you thinking that brings so fierce a look to your face?" Her soft voice broke through his angry thoughts.

Ladan turned and studied the female sitting on the ground. She was dressed in a long-sleeved royal blue coat-dress, slit up the side to the waist. Underneath, she wore a pair of powder blue loose trousers. Her only break with the traditional Geala garb was the gold circlet around her head.

She met his scrutiny with a steady expression.

"Someone betrayed me to the Dyne," he answered harshly. "What happened this afternoon was no accident."

Her eyes widened. "Do you know who might have done this evil thing?"

Someone high in the Alliance who had known of his mission had told Menoth, but Ladan decided not to share this information with her. "It's not important. What's important is getting you safely to Ezion Geber. I will deal with the traitor later."

Talia shivered at the coldness in his voice.

"Try to sleep. You will need your strength tomorrow."

Talia pulled her cloak tighter around her body. The cave was cold, but she welcomed the familiar, unchanging element. It was something familiar in her devastated world.

In spite of her best efforts, the grief over her father's death broke through her self-control, and she put her head on her knees. Her body shook with silent sobs.

When the dark storm of tears passed, her thoughts turned to the journey ahead ... and to Ladan.

The Dark Hunter.

She glanced at the man standing at the cave entrance. Dee's name fit the tall, hard, strangely handsome male. His lithe, heavily-muscled body was clothed completely in leather. In addition to the laser gun at his hip, two belts were crossed over his vest and bare chest, each holding a scabbard and knife. The intricate design worked into the black and gold hilts of the wicked blades matched the gold bands hugging his upper arms.

The dark beauty and violence that clung to him as snugly as the leather he wore both intrigued and repulsed her. Even though she had had limited contact with males—her father, Dee and his men—she knew instinctively Ladan was one of a kind.

From the first instant she sensed his presence on the stairs, he had disturbed her. When she had turned to face him, the sight of him physically jolted her.

Even now she could feel the heat of his body as he had wrestled her to the floor. For the first time since her mother died, another being had physically touched her. The pain of his bone-crushing grip around her wrist had warred with the electric shock and strange pleasure his touch created.

Unable to understand these new, churning emotions, Talia rose and joined Ladan. She looked out over the valley, trying to think of this season's crop and who would harvest it.

"What do you see, Talia?" Ladan asked, his golden eyes studying her in a disquieting way.

"I was wondering who will gather in the harvest while I am gone."

"Won't Dee do that?"

Talia laughed then blushed over her breach of etiquette. Never would she have laughed in her father's presence. Smiled perhaps, but not an open laugh. She turned and looked out over the land. "Dee and his followers are traders. I cannot see him turning farmer. I would not ask it of him."

Ladan leaned against the cave wall and winched as he was reminded of the wound on his arm. He heard Talia moan and glanced up. Her eyes were fixed on his raw flesh.

"You've never shot anyone before, have you?" he asked.

She bit her lip and shook her head. "That needs to be attended. I have salve back at the house."

"I'm fine."

"But—"

"No, Talia. Under no circumstances are we going back."

She fell silent and he could just imagine the guilt that swamped her.

"I'm surprised your father had a weapon," Ladan commented.

"He did not," she admitted guiltily. "The weapon was my mother's." Her fingers played with the fabric of her cloak. "After the air attack, I was afraid soldiers would follow. I knew where Mother had hidden the weapon. My only thought was to protect Father." She blinked and he saw the tear fall onto her cheek.

Against his will, he reached up and wiped the tear from her face. It felt like acid on his skin, burning him. "You acted as you should have. You defended yourself."

Her indigo eyes darkened. "My father would not have approved of what I did."

Ladan's harsh laugh echoed through cave. "And he would have damned you along with him. The Geala were too peaceful for their own good."

Ladan studied her stiff form. He had to ask the question burning in his gut. "Are you a telepath?"

Talia spun around, her surprise etched on her lovely face. "No, not in the sense you mean. I cannot communicate my thoughts to another simply by thinking. Nor can I read others's minds. But I can sense things that even my father, a true telepath, could not."

Intrigued, he asked, "What things?"

Her hesitation and high color told him of her embarrassment. "Emotions. I always could feel my father's emotions even though he held them under tight control. I knew what he was feeling. Sometimes I can sense an event before it happens."

"You sensed I was on the stairs earlier today."

"Yes, I knew you were there." She paused, and he could see her erecting a protective barrier.

"What else?" When she did not answer him, he grabbed her wrists and yanked her to his chest. The explosive contact surprised them both. Talia gasped. Ladan released her but did not step away. "What else?"

"There is something I cannot explain. Your presence is much stronger than anything I have ever experienced before. Usually I can tell when Dee is coming, but not all the time. With you, the current is so strong that no matter what is in my mind, your presence is felt."

Ladan ground his teeth in frustration. The female had an odd effect on him, and he didn't need to know his feeling was reciprocated. The trip to Ezion Geber would be dangerous enough without having to deal with the baser instincts this little breed aroused.

"Ladan?" Her voice broke into his thoughts. "What will I find out there beyond these mountains? I do not know what to expect. I was warned as a child not to go beyond the sheltering boundaries of this land, or it could mean my death. Were my parents right?"

The female's stilted, formal language shouted her Geala roots. "Yes, they were right. Death will stalk you because of who you are."

"Who I am?"

"That's right. Your speech, that blue star in your hand, shout to all you're Geala."

"Geala? What is that?"

A violent curse broke from his lips. "Didn't your parents tell you anything? Did they think your ignorance would protect you?" The pinched and anxious expression on her face told him that his harsh words had shocked her again. Well, if he didn't miss his guess, it would not be the last time he'd scare her on this trip. "Go to sleep. We leave at first light."

He looked out at the valley again, ignoring her. He had enough to worry about, like trying to keep them both alive until they reached Ezion Geber, the capital of the Alliance, without wasting time in polite responses. Her gentle ways be damned.

Chapter 2

Ladan rolled his head back and forth, trying to ease the tension in his shoulders. It was close to first light and he was eager to start their journey. The night had been too long.

"Tell me of the Geala," Talia asked in a soft, musical voice that made his blood race and brought lusty thoughts to his mind.

He sighed. This female was going to be trouble. "What do you want to know?"

"You said I was Geala. What is that?"

"Technically, you're only part Geala." He surveyed her golden hair, deep blue eyes, and peach-colored skin. He wondered who her mother had been. "Your father was a typical Geala with silver hair, pale eyes, and white skin. They were nicknamed Moon People."

"Moon People. Were they called this because they were so fair or for another reason?"

Ladan shrugged. "Who knows?"

"Perhaps it was because—"

"Do you want to know about your father's people or have a debate?"

She flushed. "Please continue."

He gave her a curt nod. "The Geala were an advanced race of telepaths who lived on a planet on the edge of the star system. Although mentally advanced, they were very sensitive to pain. When the leaders of the Dyne Union discovered this, they used pain to coerce them into developing a computer defense system that destroyed the rival Kanta Alliance."

Talia gasped. "That's why Father . . ." she murmured distractedly. She shook her head and her eyes refocused on him. "Go on."

"The system worked, and the Dyne became the rulers of the star system, but their cruelty was too much for the Geala. In a move that shocked everyone, one day they simply shut down the system and fled. By then the Kanta Alliance had regained enough strength to win in a one-to-one battle with the Dyne. The Dyne had to retreat back to their home planet, but they placed a bounty on the head of every Geala. As far as I know, your father was the last living member of his race."

"The Dyne will want to kill me before I can fulfill my father's wish."

The girl was quick. Ladan walked to her side, squatted down, and took her left hand. The contact jarred him, but he ignored his body's reaction. With his other hand, he pressed her fingers back to reveal the blue star in her palm. "That marks you, as it did all the other Geala, even if you are a tasha."

"Tasha? What is that?"

His mouth pulled tight in a sneer. "It's the polite way of saying you're a breed. Half-blood. Mixed race. Or a thousand other ugly names people call tashas. You're an individual who has the blood of two races but usually is accepted by neither. Who belongs to neither." He paused, shaking off bitter memories. "You are not to show that mark to anyone, do you understand?" he harshly demanded. "I can pass you off as a female of any number of other races, but if you show that palm, everyone—including the Dyne assassins—will know who you are."

She gently tugged at her hand and he released it. With her hands folded in her lap, she looked at him. "I understand and will try to conceal the mark."

"Don't try," he roared. "Do. Both of our lives depend on it."

She flinched at his tough tone. Growling in frustration, he rose and stomped out of the cave. He couldn't take any more of her innocence.

They left with the first light of day. The sand quickly grew hot. Ladan glanced over his shoulder at the small figure trudging behind him. With her body used to the high, cool valley, Ladan worried how Talia's body would endure the desert heat. She had not complained, he'd give her that. In fact, she hadn't uttered a word since they set out this morning. At the valley's entrance, she'd hesitated, then looked at him. Apparently she received whatever assurance she needed, because she started walking again.

Her trust bothered him. He was a bounty hunter, the most notorious, the most vicious of his kind. Dee had instantly recognized the danger. Everyone in the En Gedi Star System knew his reputation and feared him, except this one little Geala breed. What did she see in him that no one else for millions of lightyears around did not? Why did she trust him?

She couldn't possibly know about his reputation for honor. Once an individual or government hired him to find a criminal or to complete a mission, he bound himself to that quest and nothing stopped him. He couldn't be bought or bribed. Perhaps the female sensed this in him and felt sure he would safely deliver her to Ezion Geber.

The other thing that bothered him about Talia was her telepathic ability. If she really could read his emotions, they were in trouble. He had some very strong, basic urges concerning her, and if she read those correctly, she would probably faint.

Ladan shook off the dark thoughts and scanned the horizon. The gigantic rust-colored cloud on the eastern horizon stopped him cold.

"Why did you stop?" she panted.

He pointed toward the storm.

"What is it?" Her voice sounded small and frightened.

"A sandstorm." He looked around the barren landscape. Huge boulders rose from the desert floor, but he remembered a cluster of rocks further ahead that would provide a better shelter. He grabbed her hand and started running.

Talia's legs gave out after a few steps, and she stumbled and fell. Ladan scooped her up, threw her over his shoulder and continued. They reached the protective rocks just as the storm overtook them.

Ladan set her down, then yanked her pack from his back. "Hurry," he yelled above the howling wind, pulling her cloak from the pack. "Get under."

They huddled side by side under the dark material, but Ladan was so large the cloak failed to cover both of them. Without hesitation, he pulled the girl across his lap and pressed her face into his neck, tucking the cloak tightly around them.

Above the shrieking wind, a crack of thunder rolled. Talia jerked in his arms. Another peal sounded and she burrowed deeper against his chest.

He turned his head and spoke into her ear. "Does this planet experience electrical storms?" His lips brushed the delicate whorls of her ear.

She nodded, and her breath warmed the skin of his neck, causing an electricity within his body that mirrored that in the heavens. He cursed, damning the whole rotten planet to everlasting oblivion.

The storm within Ladan rivaled the elements around them. He wished he could jump to his feet and outrun the churning feelings the tasha stirred within, but even nature conspired against him, keeping him prisoner under her cloak.

It was then he felt her shaking and the dampness on his neck. His large, leather-encased hand slid up her spine to clasp the back of her head, while his other hand rubbed the small of her back.

"It's all right, little Geala," he murmured in her ear. "I'm here and will let nothing harm you."

He didn't know if she heard him over the wind and thunder, but her body quit trembling, and she relaxed against him.

The silence woke him. Carefully, he shifted and pulled away the protective cloak. Night. The storm had lasted the entire day. He gazed down at the small female curled in his lap. Her head rested on his shoulder and her left hand lay palm down on the bare skin revealed by his vest. The blue star in her palm burned a hole in his chest.

He grasped her hand in his and pulled it away. His eyes focused on the star in her palm. She held the entire fate of the universe in that fragile hand, and Menoth would do all in his power to stop and destroy her.

He shifted his hand slightly so his thumb could caress her palm. Suddenly, it was not enough. He wanted to peel off his leather glove and press his palm to hers. Instead, he brought her hand up to his mouth and tasted her sweet flesh. At the soft mewling sound, his eyes flew to hers. For a moment, neither moved. Finally Ladan released her hand and slid her off his lap.

He called himself a fool and numerous other unkind names while he searched through the pack for the simple wheaten bread and goat's cheese she had brought.

Without looking at her, he handed her the food. "Eat. You will need your strength. As soon as we finish, we're leaving."

"But it is night, and cold, and you have no cloak."

Ladan turned. "I can ignore the cold, and the moons will light our way. Understand, Talia, that any delay makes the Alliance weaker and the Dyne stronger. Because of the storm, we've lost almost one day's travel. I will not waste the night."

She lowered her head and nibbled her cheese. "As you wish."

He grunted his approval and resumed eating. She would be easy to handle, after all. Now, if only his suddenly wayward body would cooperate, they might make it.

* * *

Talia trailed behind Ladan, oblivious to the cold of the desert night. Instead, her head was crowded with strange, conflicting emotions over which she had no control. She'd been frightened when she left the valley's shelter, but then she looked up and saw Ladan's towering form. Somehow, she knew she'd be safe with him, that he would guard and protect her.

When the sandstorm hit, her belief had only been strengthened. Often she and her father had watched the fierce electrical storms over the desert and been awed by their beauty. Being in one, however, was quite a different experience than watching one. If she had not been in Ladan's arms, she would have bolted, running madly from the noise and terror.

The rightness of being in his arms puzzled her. She'd been taught proper respect for another being was shown by not touching ... but touching seemed pleasant. When she woke to find Ladan softly caressing her palm, the pleasure had been exquisite, making her stomach muscles contract and making breathing difficult. When he placed his lips on her skin, her heart had nearly leaped from her chest. The whimper that had escaped her lips surprised her as much as it had him.

As she walked through the cold night, she tried to block his presence from her mind but found it impossible to erect a barrier against him. It was as if there was a homing device in him, and she carried the receptor. Now that the Dark Hunter had entered her life, nothing would ever be the same. He was her destiny, and strangely enough, she accepted it.

* * *

Petar was a class two planet, inhabitable, but not able to support a large colony of beings. The barren surface was broken by a lone range of mountains where Talia lived and a large sea. There were only a handful of settlements spread out over the surface, with the largest town located at the edge of the sea.

Because of its classification, Petar was sold to Dalfex, one of the mega-corporations that provided the Alliance with basic minerals and materials. Petar's sea contained salts, minerals and ores used throughout the Alpha section of the En Gedi Star System. Also, in addition to owning the mines and towns, Dalfex was responsible for the government of the planet.

Ladan had never liked the way Dalfex ruled its colonies. It tended to let anarchy reign and only gave a cursory nod to inter-planetary law. More than once he'd ventured into Dalfex's holdings to find his prey. The corporation did not like his interference. Ladan didn't give a damn.

With the first rays of dawn, they caught sight of their destination. Ladan wished they could enter the town under the cover of darkness, but they had already lost too much time. He couldn't afford to wait another day. He stopped and turned to Talia. "I want you to stay close to me. Don't talk to anyone. Do you understand?"

"Yes."

"Your speech is a dead give away to your heritage. If we're lucky, no one will be on the streets this early."

She looked over her shoulder at the strange collection of buildings, then back at him. Her uncertainty and agitation were plain to read. "Are there many beings in the town?"

"A few. None will harm you."

Her smile seemed forced. She took a deep breath and drew herself up. A serenity, noble and proud, settled over her. He applauded her courage.

As they neared the settlement, Talia asked, "What are those structures made of? I have never seen such material."

Ladan sighed. A female taught to think, as Geala females were, was nothing but a major pain that rivaled any torture the Dyne had invented. "The buildings are constructed with a prefabricated material used commonly throughout the star system. The mineral used to produce it is mined here on Petar."

"Petar?"

"Fools," Ladan hissed, thinking of Talia's parents. They'd taught the girl only useless knowledge and kept her ignorant of the truth. "The name of this planet." His voice clearly reflected his irritation.

Talia fell silent.

Cautiously, his instincts on full alert, he entered the town. It boasted only one street. Ladan decided to skirt the back of the buildings to reach the craft landing area at the far end of the town.

Cautiously, he picked his way through the trash and debris piled behind the buildings. Nobody stopped them until they reached the last structure. Two men stepped from the shadows and placed themselves in Ladan's path.

"What do we have here?" a short, stout male asked.

"A female, you fool," the other man answered. He looked at Ladan. "Care to share her with us? We'll make it worth your while."

"No." The word rang out as deadly as one of Ladan's knives.

The second man backed away. "C'mon, Henry, let's go."

The one called Henry hesitated.

"Listen to your friend," Ladan advised. "It will save your life."

Henry's eyes narrowed. "Another time," he murmured and turned away.

Ladan didn't spare the duo another glance, but grabbed Talia's hand and headed for his ship. When he reached his vessel, he released her.

"Is that your vessel?" she quietly asked. Something in her tone alerted him to her unease.

"Yes."

"It is like the ones that destroyed my home," she uttered, dazed.

Ladan smiled coldly. "You're right. It's a Dyne fighter. I took it from an arrogant officer who crossed me the wrong way."

She stepped away from him.

"Look at me, Talia." When she refused, he reached out and cupped her chin, forcing her to meet his eyes. "Read what's in my mind. There is no betrayal. I'll deliver you safely to Ezion Geber."

She searched his eyes for several heartbeats. Then her eyes cleared of doubt and she relaxed.

"Why do you use a Dyne ship?" she asked. "Will not the Alliance mistake you for one of the enemy?"

"The outside colors are different from the Dyne and my identification beam lets the Alliance fighters know who I am."

The sleek vessel resembled a bird in flight, wings stretched. The smooth outer skin was white, its wing tips painted gold. Centered on each was an intricate design of black and gold which matched the design in his arm bands.

"What does the design represent?" Talia asked, moving closer to the ship.

"What design?" Ladan mumbled, slowly walking around the ship, running his hands over the outside.

"On the wing. Your armbands carry the same symbol, therefore it must hold a special meaning to you."

"Has anyone ever told you that you are too inquisitive?" At her wounded expression, he threw his head back and took a deep breath. "Among my father's people, each male has a design created for him at birth. All his life, everything that male owns is marked with that brand. That"—he pointed to the wing—"is mine."

"Are females accorded this same honor?"

Ladan couldn't prevent the harsh laugh that burst from his lips. "Females do not own property. They *are* property."

"That is—that is—"

"Barbaric?" Ladan offered in amusement.

She tilted her chin up in a regal fashion. "Unenlightened. Certainly any race of people who consider females property should not rule."

Ladan doubled over in laughter. He couldn't remember the last time he had laughed, but his little Geala's sense of outraged dignity amused him.

After finishing his preflight check, Ladan became aware that Talia was missing—again. No doubt her curiosity had made her careless, and she, unthinkingly, had wandered away from the protection of his ship. He jumped down from the hatch and began to look for her among the strange assortment of commercial and private vessels parked on the hard, dry land.

"Did you escape your companion?" he heard a voice wheeze as he approached an old craft.

Ladan squinted and recognized one of the men from the alley. He was struggling with someone in the vessel's shadow. The man's greasy brown hair fell into his red-rimmed eyes. Broken black and brown teeth protruded from his angry mouth.

"Release me. Ladan will—"

"The man with you was Ladan?"

Ladan sprinted forward. When he saw the fat, little man trying to subdue Talia, he wanted to kill him for even daring to touch her. The only thing that stopped him was the need to get Talia safely away from her captor first.

"Release the female." Ladan's rock-hard command startled Henry, causing him to jump away. Ladan held out his hand to Talia in silent command to come.

She had taken a step toward Ladan when Henry lunged at her. Ladan knocked Talia out of the way, drew his knife, and threw it with such force that the man staggered back several steps before falling to the ground, dead.

The soft whimper at his feet caused Ladan to glance down. Talia's eyes were fixed on the knife protruding from Henry's barrel chest. Slowly, she raised her head. The horror and anguish darkening her eyes ripped through him, angering him.

"Why? Why was it necessary for you to kill him?" Talia asked in a soft bewildered tone.

Ladan's anger came in great battering waves. He hauled her to her feet and pulled her toward the dead man.

"Look!" he commanded, his voice low and cold.

Her eyes widened as she stared at the laser gun clutched in the man's hand.

"He wanted you. And to have you, he had to kill me. Let this be a lesson to you, Talia—never, never leave my side until we reach Ezion Geber. Now, get into my ship while I hide the body. I don't want to give these so-called authorities an excuse to delay us."

Ladan quickly hid the body in an abandon space transport. When he returned to his ship, he found Talia standing beside the vessel. Her eyes held a dark, haunted look. She didn't protest when he maneuvered her through the hatch and strapped her into the co-pilot's seat. After engaging the ship's computer, Ladan contacted the tower, telling them he was ready to leave. The laser network that blanketed the planet and disrupted instruments on incoming vessel would have to be turned off in order for him to leave. The system had been set up after Dalfex discovered other companies were secretly mining the rich minerals of their planet.

"You wish to leave?" The voice answering Ladan's request held a note of surprise. Obviously the individual thought the Dyne had taken care of him.

"Is there a problem, Dalfex tower?" Ladan coldly inquired.

"Uh . . . no. Shields will be down in ninety seconds and will remain down for two minutes."

"Acknowledged, tower."

As Ladan guided his ship out of Petar's planetary pull, a single message was sent from the surface.

Prey Alive. Send Intercept!

Chapter 3

Ladan stared sightlessly at the ship's panel before him. Anger clouded his vision. What had that stupid female thought she was doing by wandering off like that? Couldn't she read the hungry stares of the two males who had laid eyes on her in that dingy town? Obviously not, he thought sourly. Talia knew nothing of the baser instincts of most races. She had been raised in an artificial world of politeness and gentleness.

He slammed his fist down on the console. Nearly one star day of the ten-day journey to the capital had passed and Talia had yet to utter a word, shocked by the death of that slime on Petar.

What else could he have done? Let the bastard kill him? He'd had no choice. But how could he explain that to her and make her understand? And how could he explain that violence was an essential part of his nature? She would never understand that he'd been raised to be ruthless. Never would she comprehend why every gentle or kind instinct he'd ever possessed had been beaten or driven from his heart. And she'd never, never understand the hatred that had filled his days, or the pain he'd experienced seeing his mother brutalized every day.

No, Talia only knew light and goodness, nothing of the harsh realities of life. He'd been her first lesson, and, oddly enough, he didn't like the idea of being the one to soil her perfect world.

Talia ran her hand over the rough material covering the bed. Ladan's presence in this small compartment was overpowering. A vest, pants, and a white shirt hung on hooks by the head of the built-in bed. His scent, clean and manly, rose from the sheets.

Rubbing her aching head, Talia tried to calm her turbulent emotions. She was pulled to Ladan on such an elemental level that she had no control over her feelings. Yet, the man himself confused and frightened her. She still could not believe how easily or quickly he had killed that man on Petar.

She drew in a deep breath and closed her eyes. *Think, Talia. Look at the situation logically as Father taught you.*

Once calm, she had to admit that Ladan had acted only in her defense. If she had not disobeyed him by wandering off by herself, then he would not have been forced to kill that man. The fault was hers. Ladan deserved an apology.

She walked to the stairs and slowly climbed the narrow, metal steps. She hesitated at the top. Her gaze moved slowly around the small cockpit, taking in the panels, equipment, and computer screen. A window above the pilot and co-pilot chairs gave her a clear view of the star system. Her eyes drifted back to Ladan, sitting in the pilot's chair. Putting aside her fear, she moved to his side.

"Ladan?"

"What?" he barked, refusing to look at her.

She sat next to him. "I am sorry for disobeying you. My actions caused you to kill that man. I am ashamed of my behavior. Father always said my nature was too willful."

Ladan heard the trembling in her soft, musical voice and turned to her. Her head was bowed, her hands tightly clasped in her lap. He caught hold of her chin and forced her to meet his eyes.

"Will you promise to obey me from now on?"

In spite of his restraining fingers, she glanced down. "Yes."

He forced her chin higher. "Talia, look at me." Timidly, her eyes found his. "I am a bounty hunter. Do you know what that is?"

"No," came the whispered reply.

"Bounty hunters are violent men who hunt the most degenerate, vicious criminals in our galaxy. We venture into those sections of the star system where there is no law and bring out the men we're paid to find." He heard her gasp but continued. "Before we arrive at Ezion Geber you will probably again be exposed to my violence. It is part of me. I cannot change. But don't be afraid. I won't hurt you."

He cupped her cheek and lightly ran his thumb over the smooth skin. "You are so soft," he murmured, his eyes caressing her face, from her high forehead adorned with a simple gold circlet to her lush mouth.

He ran his thumb over her lips. "You don't know about kissing, do you, little Geala, or the pleasures of the flesh?" He paused to see if she would react to the words. When she stared blankly at him, he continued. "A kiss is the meeting of two mouths." He lightly pulled down her lower lip to expose straight, white teeth.

"For what purpose?"

Her sweet breath flowed hotly around his thumb, and he struggled to concentrate on her question. "Purpose?"

"Kissing. What purpose does it serve?"

"To give pleasure. To receive pleasure." *To rouse passion. To sate hunger.*

"Pleasure," she murmured breathlessly.

Leaning forward he murmured, "Let me show you." His mouth gently covered hers. The fire in him wanted to devour her, to taste the honey beyond her lips, but he knew that the contact of their mouths was overwhelming her. Instead, he lightly brushed his mouth across hers.

He forced himself to pull back. Talia's face was completely blank, her eyes wide and unreadable. He muttered a foul imprecation as he turned back to the console. What idiotic impulse had possessed him to kiss her? What was it about the tasha that drove him to such rash actions? Around her he was as disoriented as the ship's guidance system after an ion storm.

Ladan glanced at Talia. She sat frozen in her chair. It appeared that every nerve, every muscle, every fiber of her being was strung so tight Ladan feared she might snap at any moment. Her eyes drifted closed and her body began to tremble.

With one single thoughtless action Ladan knew he

had smashed the brittle edges of her universe and shown her what lay beyond, what others knew and experienced.

But what disturbed Ladan most was whether she sensed the deep pleasure he'd taken from the contact of his lips upon hers. And wanted to experience again.

A loud warning beep sounded, shattering the silence. "Approaching fighters," the computer voice droned. Ladan leaned forward and scanned the heavens.

"They know about you, Talia," he said, adrenaline filling his veins. "The Dyne know about you. I count five fighters. Computer, is that correct?"

"Correct."

"Distance."

"5.3 grids."

"Time they will be within laser range?"

"Counting 12 seconds."

Ladan punched several buttons on the panel. The small screen in front of Talia's chair engaged. "The computer will track the fighters," he told her. "When the laser is locked on the target, a red light will appear at the top of the screen. All you have to do is push this button." He pointed to the square, green button at the bottom of the console.

"You want me to fire upon those vessels?" she asked, her tone full of disbelief.

Ladan grabbed her wrist and jerked her toward him. "You bet your sweet life I expect you to destroy those vessels. This is not just a matter of you killing one man. An entire empire depends on you. Now do it."

He released her and turned back to the controls. Talia stared blankly at the screen until a burst of light blinded her eyes. The ship shook as it took the opposing laser hit.

"Fire, damn it, Talia! Fire!"

Talia pressed the button, and the Dyne fighter exploded in a shower of light and metal. Ladan grunted in satisfaction.

The remaining four fighters were joined by three more. Ladan shouted a curse as he tried to maneuver his vessel around the enemy, but there were too many.

As he wove his craft between the fighters, he was amazed that his little Geala didn't shrink from her duty. In fact, the female was good, destroying or crippling two more fighters. He'd only killed four.

Feeling smug from the victory, Ladan didn't notice one of the crippled fighters turning toward them. Too late the computer warned of the incoming blast. The shot struck the aft part of the ship, hitting the engine. They lost maneuverability.

Angered that he'd been suckered, Ladan shut down all systems and patiently waited for the crippled fighter to close in for the kill. When it was within range, Ladan fired his final laser at the vulnerable belly of the Dyne ship. The beam found its target and the resulting explosion threw both Talia and Ladan to the floor.

"Are you hurt?" Ladan asked, pulling Talia to her feet. He frowned when he saw the red welt on her chin.

"No," she stammered.

Gently he helped her into the co-pilot's chair, then raced down the stairs to the deck below. Several minutes later he reappeared. His expression grim, he threw himself in the pilot's seat.

"Computer, what is the nearest habitable planet?"

"Alter 3."

"How far away is it?"

"20 grids. Arrival at this reduced speed will be in 9.7 star hours."

Ladan's golden eyes hardened and his jaw flexed.

"The black hole of this section," he growled to himself. He swung his chair around to face Talia and took both her hands in his. "That last laser blast hit the main engine. There is a smaller backup, but there's only enough fuel for it to operate for 10 star hours, which, if we meet with no difficulty, will be long enough to get us to Alter 3."

"Can the main engine be fixed?"

"Yes, but not here in deep space. Even on Alter 3 I don't know if they will have the equipment to repair the main engine, but we should be able to find some sort of transportation to Ezion Geber."

As his mind focused on the dangers ahead, he absently stroked his thumbs over the soft skin of her inner wrists.

"What are you not telling me, Ladan?" she asked quietly.

He arched his brow and looked deep into her eyes. "Tasha, are you reading my mind?"

"I can sense you are troubled."

He released her hands and laughed gruffly. "Oh, yes, I'm troubled. You see, Alter 3 is an appropriation planet, which means if you have enough coin you can buy anything you wish. *Anything*, Talia. But their main commodity—what they are famous for—is flesh. Female flesh. If a male wants to purchase a female, he comes to Alter 3 and buys one. The flesh market is very popular with Zicri."

"But what do the authorities say? Do they simply stand back and allow this to happen?"

"There are no authorities on Alter 3. No law."

"Why do the women allow themselves to be sold?" she asked indignantly.

Ladan grinned. His little Geala was going to find a lot of things in the galaxy that she would not approve of or understand. "They have no choice. They are stolen from different lands and planets and brought to Alter 3 to be sold. It is a very lucrative trade."

"And the Alliance permits this?"

"No, Talia. Alter 3 is beyond the boundaries of the Alliance, and that is the main reason I dislike having to land there. I've made enemies among the thieves on Alter 3, and they would like nothing better than to slit my throat." He pointed his finger at her. "I'm warning you right now to obey me in everything. The danger we face is great."

He punched in the coordinates for Alter 3, then leaned back. When he discovered who had betrayed him to Menoth, he would tear out his heart!

Three star hours from Alter 3, Ladan discovered a leak in the fuel line of the backup engine. According to the computer's estimate, they had lost an hour's worth of propellant. By reducing their speed further, the computer advised, he might be able to stretch their supply to make it to Alter 3.

But though he had enough fuel to enter Alter's atmosphere without burning up, there was no extra to maneuver his craft.

"Computer, send out a code 9 message to Jeiel. The last report I had, he was in this section. Give him our coordinates." He turned to Talia. "We will make the surface, but I cannot choose the landing site." He reached out and squeezed her hand. "Trust me, Talia."

Eyes calm and clear, she whispered, "I do."

With her trust affirmed, Ladan turned back to his instruments. Alter 3 was a lushly vegetated planet with three large sprawling cities and numerous smaller ones. If he had his choice he would set his craft down outside one of the larger cities, but fate and lack of fuel made that impossible.

The ship bucked and shivered entering the atmosphere, and Ladan fought to control the vessel.

"Computer, on this trajectory, where will we land?"

"Coordinates forty degrees—"

"No, damn it. Are we going to crash near any cities?"

"None on this trajectory. If you can steer two degrees negative of present course, it will place you within days of Nova Seth."

"Well, that's just dandy. How do you suggest I steer without power?"

"Is that a rhetorical question?" the computer blandly responded.

Ladan ignored the machine. Instead, he concentrated on the dense jungle spreading before them. There were no signs of civilization anywhere. With all his strength, Ladan struggled with the steering column, trying to keep them from spinning out of control.

The ship fell like a rock, branches and foliage battering the outer hull. Finally, the fighter hit the ground and skidded to a halt at the base of a small rise.

The windshield shattered upon impact. Ladan and Talia were thrown from their seats. He didn't know how long he'd been out, but when Ladan woke he was lying on the floor at the back of the cockpit. Talia was on the floor under the navigator's chair. He wiped away the blood trickling down his brow and crawled to her.

Raw fear gripped him as he stared down at her still form. He ran his hands over her limbs to make sure nothing was broken. She appeared to be all right, but Ladan knew he could not spare the time to make a thorough examination. He stood, snatched an extra laser gun from the weapons rack, then forced open the ship's door. He scooped her up and felt the wetness at the base of her skull.

He held her tighter as he staggered from the ship, wondering how much time they had before it blew. He hoped Jeiel had received his message before they descended into Alter's atmosphere. Jeiel, his old friend and fellow bounty hunter, might be his and Talia's only hope of getting to Ezion Geber.

He hurried away from the ship through the jungle until he came to a small stream. After kicking away the debris covering the ground, making sure none of the nasty little creatures who lived in the jungle of Alter were hidden there, Ladan gently laid Talia down. Kneeling beside her, he pulled the clamp from the end of her single braid and lightly ran his fingers through her hair, seeking the source of her bleeding. He found a small lump behind her left ear.

He stripped off his gloves, cupped his hands, and dipped them in the flowing water. Lightly, he dribbled water over her face, then washed the area behind her ear. Talia moaned.

His palms tingled at the unfamiliar contact as he wiped the water from her cheeks. Frowning at the gold circlet preventing him from washing her forehead, he started to remove it. Suddenly Talia's hands were on his, stopping him.

"No," she hoarsely cried.

Ladan didn't know if it was her sudden movement, her vehement denial, or the touch of her soft skin upon the rough back of his hands, but a sizzling shock zipped through him. He yanked his hands back as if burned, whirled on one knee, and put on his gloves. When he turned back to her, she was sitting, her cheeks a bright pink.

"Forgive my rudeness," she mumbled uneasily. "You startled me."

Concerned with his own secrets, Ladan failed to question her odd reaction.

"What happened?" Talia asked, trying to stand. Her knees buckled and she tumbled into Ladan. Caught off balance, he fell with her. They lay still until Ladan raised his head and said, "For a little thing, you sure carry a wallop."

Maybe it was the shock of the crash, or the ridiculous picture his words created, that someone so small could fell a man so big, but Talia began to giggle. After a moment, Ladan joined her. His laughter was deep and rich. She struggled to sit up, laying her hand on his chest to gain leverage.

Ladan's laughter died in his throat when he felt her palm upon his chest. His baser instincts roared to life.

She must have felt his reaction—and she didn't need her telepathic abilities for that—because her laughter died and slid off him. He bit back a moan.

Her cheeks turned pink with embarrassment. Ladan was sure if the ground opened up at this instant and swallowed her, she would welcome the opportunity to escape.

The tense silence that followed pulsed with sexual awareness.

"Is this the first time you have laughed?" she asked. Her curiosity overrode her embarrassment.

"No, I've laughed before." But his words carried no conviction.

"But not with true joy as you did now."

She was right, no matter how much he hated to admit it.

"I am glad I could give you that gift." She glanced around the small clearing. "Where are we? And where is your ship?"

Ladan stood, brushing the clinging leaves from his pants. "I left the ship a distance back. If we were tracked by the Dyne or someone from the surface, they might send someone out to investigate. I want to get to Nova Seth unnoticed. As to where we are, we are probably six or seven day's walk from Nova Seth in the middle of Alter 3's jungle."

"The situation does not sound encouraging."

"Our chances of making it to Ezion Geber are about one in ten. But I've faced worse odds before, Talia, and lived to tell about it."

Talia's lips curved up in what might have been a grin. "Well, I am comforted to know at least one of us knows what he is doing."

He pulled the extra laser gun from inside his vest and handed it to her. "Keep this with you at all times. Don't hesitate to use it. Our lives might depend on your quick reaction. And do not stray from my side again."

"I understand, and will do as you wish."

She looked at him, and he sensed she understood the fierce determination that drove him, that he would let nothing stop him from completing this mission.

Jeiel stroked his golden beard as he studied the star chart before him. Now where could the renegade Mythian officer find shelter in this sector?

The ship's computer beeped, notifying Jeiel of an incoming message.

The tall bounty hunter looked up. "What is it, Sarah?"

"I have a code 9 message coming in," the computer answered.

Jeiel leaned back in his chair. "From whom?"

Chapter 4

As they trudged through the steaming jungle, Talia wondered why Ladan had not questioned her odd reaction to the removal of the circlet from her forehead. She hoped he would forget the entire incident, because if he asked about it, she did not know how she would answer. She could not tell him the truth, yet lying was beyond the realm of possibility. She could not simply omit telling him the truth because her Geala upbringing prevented even that small twist of the truth.

Talia forced herself to move forward. Her head throbbed. The wet heat of Alter 3 was clinging to her like sticky tentacles wrapped around each of her limbs, holding her back, making every step a battle. Father, of course, would have demanded a more accurate and scientific description of the situation.

Thoughts of her father brought guilt. Her behavior since she had left home had been unseemly. Her reaction to Ladan was highly improper, but each time he touched her, strange things happened to her. Her eyes focused on the black-clad figure in front of her. He moved through the dense foliage soundlessly, with the lithe, rhythmic grace of an Enoran mountain cat.

You don't know about kissing, do you, little Geala, or the pleasure of the flesh? Ladan's words ran through her head.

Kissing.

Touch.

Contact.

Pleasure.

Electricity!

The instant his lips had touched hers, it was like a super-nova exploding inside her, knocking her universe off its axis, leaving her without a sense of direction. He was a forbidden fire that would consume her if she allowed him to kiss her again. And yet, wasn't fire a purifying agent that burned the dross from precious metal?

Shocked by the thought, she turned her mind to the battle with the Dyne fighters. Again, her actions had surprised and disturbed her. An instinct, one that she had never known, had sprung to life in her from deep within. She had battled the Dyne right along with Ladan and found satisfaction in winning.

It occurred to her that Ladan was the catalyst of all her new and utterly shameless behavior. He saw into the dark side of her nature, the side she had never been able to experience under Geala rule.

What he had said about being a tasha was right. All her life she had tried to maintain the standards her father had set, but there was something inside her that could not abide by his strict rules. At times, it was like she was two different beings, and those two were constantly at war. She was both—yet neither. Somehow, Ladan knew what it was to be a tasha.

The air seemed to grow thicker. She stopped and took a deep breath. If she could get some air into her lungs, she could continue. Talia's eyes drifted closed. *Reach deep and gather your strength. Do not let the situation control you. Rise above these hardships.* She could hear her father reciting this litany.

Reassured, she opened her eyes and starting walking. She'd taken only a few steps when her leg muscles cramped, forcing her to stop.

"Ladan," she called out as she leaned against a thick tree. The bark under her shoulder squeaked. Talia jerked upright to stare into the red eyes of a small, oval-shaped reptile with bony spines running down his back. The brown creature squeaked again and launched itself at her.

Ladan heard Talia's call, and turned in time to see the creature jump from the tree. It bounced off Talia's shoulder and landed on the ground. She didn't shriek or yell or jump. She simply closed her eyes and soundlessly collapsed. How anyone could fall in such a dignified manner was beyond him, but she had accomplished the feat. Proper to the end. Just once he'd like to see her lose control and give into the passion he sensed beneath her cool exterior.

He plucked the little fellow from the ground by Talia's head and crouched down. "You should be ashamed of yourself," he scolded the animal. "She didn't know you are completely harmless." Tucking the creature under his arm, he lightly tapped Talia on the cheek.

"Come on, little Geala. Wake up."

Groggily, Talia became aware of her surroundings. "Ladan?"

HUNTER'S HEART

"Right here, Talia."

"What happened?" She opened her eyes. The sight of the thing in Ladan's arms froze her.

"You fainted."

"What?" she mumbled, distracted by the animal's red eyes.

"You fainted."

His words finally pierced the numbness surrounding her brain, and Talia closed her eyes as a wave of humiliation washed over her. She had disgraced herself again.

"How are you feeling?" Ladan asked.

"Fine," she muttered.

Ladan's eyes narrowed. "There is something else, isn't there, Talia. What's wrong? What aren't you telling me?"

"I fainted. It was a most inappropriate response to the situation."

Ladan couldn't help grinning. "I assure you, Talia, you fainted in a most dignified fashion. I'd challenge anyone to find fault with your proper Geala response."

His words helped. She felt less a fool. "What is that thing?" she asked, pointing to the little creature.

"A catwig. He is completely harmless."

Talia's large indigo eyes told him she didn't believe him. "Then why did it attack me?"

"Logical to the end, aren't you? I think this poor little catwig was more frightened of you than you were of him. He was probably trying to get away." Ladan lightly scratched the animal under its chin. A squeaky purr came from the creature's chest. "See, he's as docile as the Anteran dog. Here, hold out your hands."

She complied, and Ladan placed the catwig in her hands. Immediately, Talia sensed the creature's peaceful, gentle nature. She cradled it next to her breast and stroked it. The catwig's purr started again.

"The poor little thing. It is so ugly that no one would guess that it's harmless."

"That prickly hide serves a purpose. It keeps the kelser and other predators away."

Talia glanced up. The emotions coloring Ladan's words swamped her. He was hurting. Deep inside there was a raw wound. Somehow, Ladan identified with the catwig's situation of outward appearance having nothing to do with what was inside. She started to reach out, but Ladan jerked away and stood.

"We need to find water and shelter before nightfall."

She set the catwig down and rose. As she started after Ladan, she heard a little noise. Turning, she saw the catwig scrambling after her.

"It seems you have acquired a pet," Ladan murmured in her ear.

Her startled gaze flew to his. "Really?"

"I'm afraid so." Ladan sighed. "Pick him up. We'll make better time that way."

Absurdly pleased, Talia picked up her new friend and started after Ladan.

Talia stumbled to a halt. She reached for a nearby tree, but before she could grab a limb Ladan's hands caught her arms, and he jerked her away.

"Little fool, don't you ever learn?" he spat out. "Didn't the experience with the catwig teach you anything? This jungle is crawling with animals, most of them deadly and dangerous, not like your new pet." He took her face between his hands and turned her to a tree ten meters ahead of them. "Do you see the kelser hanging from the tree branch?"

Talia instantly located the creature. The slimy red and yellow snakelike reptile seemed to be looking back at her. The creature's yellow eyes glowed as it held her mesmerized while its long, forked tongue hissed a warning.

Ladan pulled the laser gun from his belt, aimed, and fired. The creature screamed and fell to the ground. Talia shivered.

"The kelser is the deadliest creature inhabiting the jungles of Alter 3. One bite, and a grown male my size dies instantly."

His harsh recital had the desired effect on Talia. Her eyes grew round and her lower lip trembled. It was then that Ladan noticed Talia's flushed and perspiring face.

"Stupid female," Ladan growled in frustration. He snatched the catwig from her arms and set it on the ground. Gathering a handful of the green material near the top of her sleeve, he yanked. The sleeve parted from the bodice of the coat-dress. He threw the material on the ground.

"What are you doing?"

"Shut up and stand still." He roughly removed her other sleeve. Withdrawing one of his blades, he stared at her high collar. "Undo your top." Three simple fasteners of braided loops and buttons ran from the center of her neck to her right shoulder, securing the overlapping sections of the dress.

"Ladan?"

He heard the trembling in her voice, and some of his anger subsided. "You have on too much. This is not the cool mountain valley of Petar, Talia. Your clothing is keeping in your body heat. Soon, if you don't remove some of it, you'll pass out from heatstroke. Now, all I want to do is cut away your collar. Trust me, Talia, this is for your own good."

Slowly her fingers rose to the first closure at her throat. When she finished, he slid his hand under the slick material below her chin. Immediately, his mind registered how soft her skin was. Shoving aside the thought, he poked a small hole in the fabric. Replacing his weapon, he gave the collar a hard yank. It tore neatly from the dress.

He eyed his work critically. She still had on too much. It was going to wreak havoc with his baser instincts, but more of her skin needed to be exposed. He reached up and tucked under the top edges of her dress, revealing an off-center vee of white skin. It was not the pasty white color of a true Geala, but a glowing pearly-peach. Talia jerked as his fingertips brushed her bare skin. Quickly he stepped away.

He frowned at her loose pants. She could not remove them since the coat dress was split up to her waist. He knelt before her. "Give me your leg, Talia." When she hesitated, he patted his thigh. "Place your foot here."

The awkward position and her wobbly legs forced her to grab Ladan's shoulders. This was killing him, Ladan grimly thought as he cut away the pant-leg above the knee—a subtle torture meant to drive him mad. As he set her foot on the ground, he heard Talia gasp. Glancing up, he saw her face was redder than before and her eyes stared straight ahead. This was probably the first time anyone had seen her bare leg. He wished he could spare her this embarrassment, but her health demanded this action. He finished the other pant leg and rose.

More needed to be done. Ladan slowly evaluated her from her slippered-feet to the crown of her golden head.

Her hair fell loosely around her shoulders, reaching almost to her waist. He picked up one of the discarded sleeves and tore a strip from it.

"Braid your hair," he commanded, handing her the material.

Ladan watched quietly for several minutes while Talia wrestled with her thick hair. Exasperated with her clumsiness, he batted aside her hands, gritting his teeth against the riot of desire that flooded him. Her hair was as soft as moonbeams, fragrant as the air of her high valley. With quick efficiency, he parted her hair into three sections and began weaving the strands in and out.

"Where did you learn to braid hair?" Talia asked, her voice huskier than usual.

She felt the attraction, too. Suddenly, he was angry with her. Angry that she stirred these feelings in him. Angry that he could not act on his instincts. No, he couldn't touch her, for he was keenly aware of the price she would pay. "As a youth I learned how to braid whips. This is no different."

"Whips?"

"You know what they are, don't you?"

His sharp mocking made her flinch. "Yes."

He held out his hand, and she placed the torn strip in his palm. "My father's people used whips. It was considered a highly-favored skill to be able to create a good one." He felt her trembling, but his ire goaded him on. "Some threaded metal studs into the leather, but I never saw the necessity for such. If you made the whip tight enough, it would cause the intended pain."

Talia swayed. Ladan caught her shoulders and turned her around to face him. He forced her chin up. The revulsion in her wide eyes cut across his heart. Smiling bitterly, he ran his fingers over her cheek. "You can't comprehend that kind of violence, can you, Talia?"

"No." A single tear slid from the inside corner of her eye, down her cheek, falling on her lips.

He wanted to taste that tear, wanted to devour the lips it flavored. "It's the one thing all beings have in common."

"You are wrong, Ladan."

"Oh, my well-traveled tasha knows all about the star system from her brief sojourn." He dropped his sarcasm. "After recent events, you should've learned that violence reigns."

"The Creator placed in us all the desire for peace and good. Some deny and turn away from the instinct, but it is still there."

"More Geala teaching," he sneered.

"Yes."

He had heard this before and seen the teacher beaten to death. The words were false. "You're a fool."

"Perhaps, but I am a fool with hope," she gently answered.

They traveled through the jungle until they came to a small pond. The sky was turning red and Ladan did not want to risk going on with the night closing in. By the pond stood a daffus tree, its purple fruit sweet and tasty. Ladan cleared the debris from a small area out in the open away from any trees, then gathered a handful of daffus fruit. He cut the round fruit and silently handed Talia a large piece. They had not spoken to each other since their sharp exchange.

Talia sat in a cross-legged position across from Ladan. His gaze strayed to her shapely, bare calves. He seriously

HUNTER'S HEART

regretted having to alter Talia's clothes. If the temptation she presented hadn't been strong enough before, it was now impossible to ignore.

"This is delicious."

Talia's voice broke into his wayward thoughts. His head jerked up, just in time for him to see her take another bite of the fruit. A drop of juice oozed from between her lips, falling on her chin. Ladan focused on that well-shaped, pink mouth. His mental picture of the Geala would never be the same after this.

Slowly, he took in the rest of her features, her straight nose, delicate cheekbones, and high-arched golden brows that drew attention to her deep blue eyes. Her forehead was smooth and clear, always adorned with the simple vee-shaped circlet. He frowned, remembering her odd reaction when he started to remove it.

Talia instantly sensed where Ladan's thoughts had turned. The harsh planes of his face hardened and his golden eyes, with their odd diamond-shaped pupil, bore into her. She could not let him ask the question.

"Tell me about the Kanta Alliance," Talia abruptly asked.

Ladan frowned. "What do you want to know?" He threw aside the remains of his fruit. The catwig waddled over to the rind and nibbled on it.

"If they fight the Dyne, then they must be good, right?"

"Good versus evil. Is that it, Talia?"

"Yes, that is what I mean."

"Have you ever thought perhaps the Kanta Alliance is evil just like the Dyne? One evil empire fighting for power against another."

"But you would not work for them if they were evil," she quickly replied.

"I would work for anyone who was against the Dyne. Anyone."

"No, I do not believe you. I sense the Kanta Alliance is good and that the words you speak are only meant to punish me."

Her insight astounded him. And his desire to taunt her reminded him of another who acted with cruelty. As hardened as he was, he vowed not to repeat the pattern. "You are right about the Alliance, but do not underestimate my hatred for the Dyne."

He rubbed the back of his neck. "The Alliance is made up of a federation of nine planets, all democracies, including various degrees of autonomy for women. Except one."

"Names, Ladan. I wish to know the names of these democracies."

She smiled brightly at him, and he realized she was attempting to tease him. It was a unique experience which made him forget his earlier anger. He cleared his throat and thoughtfully tapped his finger against his lips. His actions caused Talia to laugh.

"Let me see if I can remember all the names. Alcor, Mizar and Cetras are in the omicron section of the star system. Fornax, Quinten, Sor and Mythen are in the delta sector. The Theams group which revolves around a double star is in the xi sector. Ditan is in the alpha sector, close to Petar. The Ditans were originally members of the Dyne Union. When the old emperor died, his son replaced him and pulled out of the Dyne Union. Marshall Usan and his daughter Kami were able to convince the new emperor to join the Alliance. The Alliance permitted this one instance of authoritarian rule because the Ditans are fierce warriors and the Alliance needed their help to defeat the Dyne."

"Then, I presume all the members of the Dyne Union are despots, tyrants, or dictators."

"Despots," he chuckled and shook his head. "I like that word. Your assumption is correct. There is no freedom for the masses in the Dyne Union," he grimly told her.

"How many members are in the Union?"

"Now, with the defection of Ditan, there are seven. Darka, the home planet of the Dyne, is located at the far end of the mu sector. Farqas and Usol in the delta sector. Trifid and Beneda in the beta. Gimiti and Hathan in the psi sector."

"And on what planet is Ezion Geber located?"

Ladan leaned over and drew a large circle in the wet soil. "The star-system is divided into twenty-four equal sections." He marked them off. "Ezion Geber is located on planet Gemmal, which is in the exact center of the circle. Gemmal is where the Geala once lived. When the Dyne found them many years ago, they had the Geala construct the computers on their home planet. Since then, it has been the capital of the star system."

The information that Gemmal was her father's home planet should have excited her, but oddly enough it did not.

"Would you like to know what Gemmal is like?" Ladan asked.

"No."

Her odd reaction surprised Ladan. "Why? I thought you would be bursting with curiosity as you normally are."

Talia's eyes seemed to focus on something on the distant horizon. "I cannot explain it. At this moment, I feel no pull to Gemmal. I want my mind free of any vision of it so when we approach it, my feelings will be pure and unbiased." Abruptly, she stood and looked around at the surrounding bushes. As she started toward a thick clump of bushes, Ladan rose.

"Where are you going?"

She did not turn around. "I need a moment of privacy." Her voiced sounded strained.

"What—" Suddenly, he understood her problem. "Be careful. Watch for kelsers." He smiled as he watched her stiff back disappear into the darkness. When she returned, she found him stretched out on the ground, his head pillowed on one arm. He patted the space beside him.

"Come, lie here."

Talia's eyes grew large, and she stepped back. "I cannot."

Ladan had expected this response. He sat, resting an arm on his upraised knee. "There are creatures in this jungle that could crawl into this area while we sleep. I am a light sleeper. If you are a great distance from me, any animal could creep up on you, and I would not hear it until it was too late. I will set the catwig between us if that eases your mind."

He counted on her pledge to obey him. Counted on her logical mind telling her that he'd been right before and was right now. She knew nothing of this jungle, and he was only trying to protect her. He saw the nervousness and fear in her eyes and guessed his nearness caused her distress.

He waited, not daring to breathe. Finally, she knelt at his side and stretched out, but she faced away from him.

Talia heard Ladan lie back down. The catwig snuggled in the arch of her back and began to purr. She breathed

Chapter 5

The dark, heavy heat of the Alteran night pressed in on Ladan, giving him no relief from the slow burning fire inside his gut. He glanced at Talia. She had turned and now faced him. The red glow of the moon bathed her sleeping form, giving her an other-worldly appearance.

She was beautiful. And he wanted her. Wanted to possess that soft, fragrant body. Wanted to touch the golden glow of her spirit. Everything about her pulled at him. He knew her, knew her ways, and he also knew that being with him would destroy that golden glow. He'd watched it happen before. He would not allow it to happen again.

Not used to denying his sexual urges, Ladan rolled away from Talia and rose to his feet. The little catwig stirred and looked up at him.

"Guard her," he admonished the creature. The catwig would squawk loudly if a kelser or any other deadly a sigh of relief. She had successfully diverted him from asking about her circlet. Her secret was still safe.

Although she couldn't see him, Talia's senses and consciousness were filled with Ladan. He was an overwhelming, vital force that was slowly pulling her away from everything she knew and loved, plunging her into a strange and unfamiliar universe. And there was nothing she could do to stop it.

head bowed. He knew what she was doing. Some races called it praying; the Geala called it taum.

The catwig scurried from Talia's side to circle Ladan's feet. The sound drew Talia from her quiet.

"I've always found it strange that an advanced people like the Geala felt a need to communicate with the Creator." Ladan knelt and handed her a slice of cut fruit.

"Father always said the more he learned, the more in awe he was of the beauty and complexity of the universe. It was fitting to thank the Being who created it."

"And what of the evil that forced your father to hide on that barren piece of rock?"

Her eyes turned dark. His blunt words had wounded her, and, surprisingly, he felt her pain as if it were his own.

"I have no answer for you. I only know where my strength lies," she softly answered.

He turned away, disgusted with himself. He was living up to his reputation of the harshest bounty hunter in the star system.

"How are you feeling this morning?" he asked, biting into his slice of daffus.

"I am fine." The deep purple shadows beneath her eyes loudly proclaimed her exhaustion.

"I wish we could go slower and allow you time to rest, but time is running out."

Her sad smile touched a tender spot in his heart, a spot he thought hardened. "I know." The catwig purred and its short legs pawed the ground. Talia grinned at the animal's antics and gave him the last of her fruit.

Ladan stood and pulled Talia to her feet. "Why don't you wash your face and hands before we leave?"

HUNTER'S HEART

animal wandered into the clearing. Ladan strode to the pond, stripped, and dove into the warm water. He wished the temperature was twenty degrees colder. It might provide him some relief.

As he washed with sand from the bottom of the pond, Ladan forced himself to think of the problems he and Talia faced. First and foremost, had the Dyne fighters signaled their home base before they'd been destroyed? He'd bet that they had. He would act accordingly, being extra cautious and alert.

Second, had Jeiel received his distress signal? He hoped so, but knew he couldn't count on the slim hope of help arriving. What had to be done to save Talia would be done by him, and him alone.

He worried about Talia's physical strength. If she had been pure Geala, he doubted she would have made it this far. Probably for the first time ever, being a breed had an advantage. How ironic. He wished he knew to what race her mother belonged.

He was also concerned about Talia's mental state. Her peaceful world had been abruptly shattered, and she had been thrust into the roiling cauldron of war and savagery. In the last few days, she had endured a thousand new feelings and experiences, yet been given no time to absorb or adjust to them. He wished he could give her the time she needed to find her bearings, but their circumstances made that option impossible.

He shook off the water and dressed. He hoped they could reach Nova Seth in three star days, but his estimate could be off by days, and every hour Talia had to suffer this crippling heat lessened her chances of survival.

He picked some daffus fruit on his way back to the clearing. When he arrived, he found Talia sitting, her

"Thank you," she whispered.

Watching her hurry toward the pond, Ladan knew he would have to keep a sharp eye on her today and not allow her to overextend herself. If necessary he would carry her to Nova Seth rather than allow any harm to come to her.

"How do you know what direction we are walking?" Talia asked during one of their numerous rest stops. "With all these trees and brushes, I cannot tell east from west."

Ladan laughed and looked around. He pulled Talia over to a short bush growing by the side of a massive tree. "Do you see the small yellow flowers on that bush? They bloom only in the morning hours and always the blooms face west. Since I know that Nova Seth is directly west of where we landed, I look for that bush and know I'm going in the right direction."

"Your knowledge is amazing," she exclaimed, delight in her voice.

"Not so amazing when you consider I've been on Alter 3 before," he ruefully replied.

Once they resumed walking, Talia scanned the jungle for the bush Ladan had pointed out. Spotting one several meters from the path, Talia scurried toward it, eager to confirm her find. The ground beneath her feet looked sound. Only when her foot plunged through the vines did she realize her mistake.

"Ladan!" she cried as she tumbled into the hole.

He whirled around. When he could not find her he became alarmed. "Talia, Talia, where are you?" he called, retracing his steps. "Damn it, woman, answer me!"

He stopped and listened, willing her to respond. His eyes scanned the ground, looking for some clue as to where his errant little Geala had wandered. He should beat her blue for her disobedience. He was certain she'd wandered off the path. But why?

He paused to listen again. He heard a small moan, then the catwig's distressed cry. The sound led him to a large opening in the ground. He could see Talia's crumpled form at the bottom of a long slope.

Slowly he walked down the incline, testing each step, hoping the ground would not shift beneath his weight.

"Ladan?"

"Right here, little Geala." He carefully surveyed the darkness beyond her. Satisfied there was no danger, he knelt by her head. "You disobeyed me, didn't you, Talia?"

She nodded. "I was looking for that bush you pointed out. I did not see the hole."

Ladan was torn between relief and anger. "Does anything hurt?"

"My ankle."

He cradled her small foot in his hand. Already the flesh was starting to swell. "Anything else?"

"No."

He ran his eyes over her body. When no further signs of injury were evident, he scooped her up in his arms.

"Wait," she cried as he started to rise. "The catwig."

He paused and allowed her to grab the little animal before he stood and strode up the incline. Once he reached the top, he didn't set her down but continued to walk through the jungle.

"I seem to have a distinct ability to get myself in trouble," Talia murmured to the stone-faced man carrying her.

His firm lips turned up slightly at the corners. "An understatement."

"I would not wish to brag upon my talent."

Ladan's brow arched, then his chest rumbled with laughter. "Tasha, your other half is showing."

Talia rested her head on his powerful shoulder. "Yes, I know. Father never appreciated my humor."

"Did your mother?"

Her brow knitted into a frown. "I cannot remember. She died when I was six."

"And what is your age now?"

"I have lived through twenty complete cycles of the seasons on my home planet."

"Let's see. Petar's year is 347 star days, and a standard star year is 400 star days, making you—"

"17.35 star years," Talia interrupted.

Ladan's expression darkened. *Much too young to be ravished by a bounty hunter starting his twenty-eighth star year,* he thought.

"Do you know to what race your mother belonged?"

"No."

A muscle contracted in his jaw. "That doesn't surprise me, since your parents avoided all contact with the truth."

"That is not fair, Ladan. My parents did only what they thought was right. I cannot fault them for that."

"And in the end, your ignorance might kill you," he snapped. "If you are part Alcoran or Mythen you can endure this heat for a long time without suffering any ill effect. If your mother was Mizan or Ditan, the heat will kill you within days. But since I have no inkling to your heritage, I'm left to wonder how long you have before you collapse."

She stiffened in his arms. "Although I am unused to

the humidity, I will survive. You need not worry about me."

His bark of laughter was harsh. "You're right, because I plan to carry you all the way to Nova Seth."

Ladan did not stop until the light faded from the sky. Even then he walked until he found a small pond. Setting Talia on an overhanging rock, he removed her slipper.

"Soak that ankle while I search for something to eat," he commanded.

Talia felt the most unnatural urge to pick up a stone and throw it at his retreating back, but then decided against the foolishness. She eased her foot into the bubbling water, not surprised at its warmth. The pond was probably heated by the geothermal activity deep beneath the planet's surface. She would like to explore the spring, discover the heat source, and map its topology, but she had already wandered off once today and nearly killed herself.

She did not hear him return, but suddenly she felt his presence behind her. He did not speak, refusing to announce his presence in any way. It was as if he wanted to study her unobserved.

"You knew I was here, didn't you?" he said as he settled on the rock by her side. His arms were filled with several strange fruits she had never seen before.

"Yes."

Ladan shook his head. "I'm glad you're not the enemy because I never would have been able to catch you by surprise."

"Oh, I do not know." Talia's eyes twinkled. "You

have given me more surprises in the last two days than I have ever had in my entire life."

Ladan winked. "I don't doubt it, little Geala. I don't doubt it."

He picked up a long, thin green fruit and pulled away the skin to reveal the white interior and handed it to her.

Cautiously, Talia took a bite. The fruit was tangy, a sensual delight to her tongue. "What is this?"

"Malow. And this"—he held up a brown root—"is gar. You strip off the outer skin and suck the juice from the inside."

Talia peeled the gar root just as Ladan had shown her. Gingerly, she raised it to her lips.

Ladan watched in fascination as her tongue darted out to taste the exposed flesh of the gar. He nearly groaned aloud at the explosive thoughts her innocent actions triggered.

"This is good," she commented between bites.

Ladan closed his eyes and tried to think of something besides Talia's lips and tongue. Feeling the desperate need to walk off his tension, he sprang to his feet.

Talia looked up at his towering form. "Is something wrong?"

Her naivete was killing him. "I'll give you several minutes alone to take care of your personal needs." He swiftly moved away from the pond, eager to escape the passion that threatened to break his self-control.

He gave Talia more time than he had planned. The tension in him didn't ease quickly, and it took a long time for him to regain his composure.

Ladan!

He heard the desperate cry and bolted back toward the pond.

The scene that greeted him when he reached her made his blood run cold. Talia stood under a tree, and hanging from the branch above her was a kelser. Its glowing red eyes held her mesmerized while its long, forked tongue hissed a warning.

"Don't move, Talia," Ladan softly commanded. He pulled the laser gun from his belt and fired. The creature's head exploded, raining bits and pieces of flesh and fluid onto Talia's face.

She didn't scream, cry, or run. She simply stared wide-eyed at Ladan.

"It's all right, Talia," he reassured her, moving to her side. "Everything is fine."

Her fingers shook as she raised them to touch her sticky cheek. Ladan's hand clamped around her wrist, stopping her.

"Don't," he commanded in a sure, strong voice.

She will panic if she touches that blood. Ladan's thoughts sizzled through Talia's mind. She didn't know what shocked her the most, his thoughts or the fact she read them so clearly.

Ladan didn't release his grip on her wrist, but pulled her toward the water. He coaxed her onto a boulder, stripped the leather gloves from his hands, then tenderly washed her face.

Her eyes never left his while he worked. When he finished, he cradled her face between his palms.

"Talk to me, Talia."

Talia saw his lips move, but failed to hear his words. Instead her mind focused on the burning center of his left palm where it touched her cheek.

A blue star.

He was Geala. He was also a tasha, like her. It explained much.

She placed her hands over his. Ladan jerked away from her. Undeterred, she reached out for his left hand. "Let me see."

Her eyes locked with his, and silently she told him she knew his secret. He allowed her to turn over his hand. Although fainter than hers, she saw the blue star in his palm.

She raised her eyes to his. "You are a tasha."

"I was never called a tasha," he replied bitterly. "Bastard, breed, half-blood. A million other hate-filled names aimed to wound and disgrace, but never tasha."

"Tell me of your mother."

"You can read too damn much, Talia." He stood and walked along the edge of the pond.

"Is that why you wear those gloves?" Talia asked.

"No." He untied the throng around his head and pushed back his black hair. Kneeling before her, he held out his clenched fists. "Do you see the scaling, Talia? Across my forehead, on the back of my hands? If anyone saw them, they would know to what race I belonged, and I want to hide that shame. I want no one to associate me with the bastard who sired me."

She was afraid to ask the next question. Afraid of his answer. He must have read the fear in her eyes because he answered her silent question.

"My father's people are the Dyne."

"That is not possible," she choked. "If that were true then—"

He reached out and caught her upper arms. She flinched. "I will not harm you, Talia. You know that. Look deep inside yourself and read the truth."

He was right. She trusted him without question or waver. The striking fear retreated, allowing her rational mind to take over. "Why do you fight against your own?"

"Because of my mother, Talia. A kind, beautiful woman who was beaten to death by my father. He married her out of spite and the laws made it impossible for her to refuse him. The Geala had thwarted him, so he took a Geala wife, and vented all his frustrations and anger on her. To be sure I exhibited none of her gentle qualities, he beat and humiliated me. I saw most of the beatings he gave my mother. He wanted that. It was easy to hurt her since the Geala are so sensitive to pain. Sometimes he would pinch her to cause her agony. Or twist her arm. Or kick her."

"Stop, Ladan," she pled, tears streaming down her cheeks.

But he seemed not to hear her. Words and emotions he'd never allowed to surface erupted.

"The day she died I was with her. She was reading to me. My father caught her. He raped her before my eyes, then beat her to death. I held her in my arms while she struggled for her final breath. Her last words were a blessing, asking the Creator to care for her son. She asked that I be given the love she would not be able to give me because her life was so short.

"I was fourteen at the time, but at that moment I vowed I would kill my father. I hid aboard a cargo vessel and have never gone back to Darka. I will one day."

"Why did your mother not leave him?" Talia softly questioned, puzzled that such a gentle female would stay with so brutal a man.

Ladan's eyes filled with disdain as he gazed at her. "You know nothing of yourself, do you?" He sighed and shook his head. "Of course you don't.

"Although the Geala were a mentally advanced race, they retained certain primitive characteristics. They took only one mate. With the first mating, some strange, unique bond was established—a bond so strong that only death would break it. My father knew this, and he never worried about my mother leaving him."

"Did this bonding work even if the other mate was not Geala?" Talia's mind focused on her father.

"Yes."

Ladan's explanation solved many of the mysteries that surrounded her parents, questions that she had long wondered about suddenly had answers.

Talia glanced down at Ladan's hands. She knew he felt the scaling was much uglier and more repulsive than it actually was. There was a slight ridge across his forehead and on the backs of his hands, but years of hiding his heritage had almost erased the harsh skin. Her fingers trailed over his left hand.

He had left out the most important part, she suddenly realized as she touched him. Meeting his gaze, she asked, "Who is your father?"

"Menoth, the head of the Dyne Union."

Chapter 6

Oddly enough, his announcement did not come as a surprise.

"Why don't you run screaming from me?"

Her brow arched. "With this ankle?"

He chuckled. "You're slipping, little Geala. Your unknown half is showing."

"I know," she whispered, her head bowed.

Ladan's violent curse made her jump. "Two star days with me, and I'm already corrupting you."

"No," she cried, reaching out to grasp his wrist. Shocked by her own boldness, she pulled her hand back. "The humor was always there. You just encourage me to speak it aloud."

His fingers lightly stroked her cheek. "Have you always fought your impulses?"

Her eyes locked with his. "You know I have," she answered solemnly. "You have spoken of the dilemma a tasha faces. Your words were true. I loved my father, but I was never able to live up to the standards he set." She paused, fighting the rising tide of emotions crashing in on her.

When she spoke again, she was surprised her voice did not betray her turmoil. "Since I left the valley, I have behaved in a manner that puzzles me. I have discovered things about myself that shock and disturb me. I am lost, Ladan. I no longer know who I am."

"Talia," he breathed, her name a sweet sound upon his lips. He pulled her into his arms and rocked her.

Turning her face into his shoulder, she fought her tears. Her attempt failed.

"Forgive my lack of con—trol," she said afterwards, wiping away the moisture on her cheeks. The tiny hiccup broke her last word, ruining her dignified apology.

"There is nothing to forgive. You have dealt well with the new things you've experienced these last days. A weaker person would have buckled under their weight. I think your father would have been proud of you and understood your need for tears."

It was a kind lie. She knew her father would not understand, but Ladan's effort to comfort her touched her.

He settled himself comfortably against a rock, shifting Talia to his side. "Go to sleep, little one."

She sighed and snuggled close. The catwig, who had hidden under a bush at the sight of the kelser, settled at their feet.

"Why were you not frightened, Talia, when I told you who my father was?"

"Because I sense I am safe with you. I have felt that way from the first moment I saw you."

"You should be afraid of me, Talia. I learned my father's lessons well."

"And your mother's, too."

Ladan look down into her face. "What do you mean?"

"My cry for help, Ladan, never passed my lips. I only called to you in my mind."

"You're wrong," he harshly replied. "I distinctly remember hearing your call."

"Think, Ladan. Recall the incident in your mind."

He closed his eyes, focusing on the instant he heard her cry. Panic seized him. She was right. He had only heard it in his mind. "That can't be. I'm not telepathic."

"Neither am I, but after you shot the kelser, your thoughts were open to me. I heard them as surely as if you had spoken them." Reading the skepticism in his eyes, she said, "You were worried that I would panic if I touched the blood on my cheek."

He pulled her back into his arms, nudging her head down onto his shoulder. "What happened was probably a freak occurrence induced by the trauma of the moment. Close your eyes, Talia, and rest. You'll need your strength for tomorrow."

In her heart, Talia knew what had happened was no freak accident, but the beginning of a bond between her and Ladan. She would not press him now by arguing the point. She closed her eyes and yielded to the peace his arms brought.

Ladan woke with the first dawning light of morning. He relived yesterday's events again, trying to deny what he knew was true. He'd heard Talia's scream telepathically. Never had he shown any tendency in this area. Why now? Why here? Why with Talia?

Nothing of his mother's Geala heritage had ever manifested itself before in his life. Did it make sense that if

Talia, a tasha, had a certain telepathic ability, that he, also, would possess that same talent? He shook his head. Even if true, the budding seed had been killed long ago by his father. How, then, could he explain yesterday?

His gaze roamed over the sleeping female at his side. He smiled ruefully. No matter how many times he warned himself that touching her would only lead to disaster, he found excuses to hold her.

His large, powerful hands skimmed over Talia's back and down her arms. Ladan liked the feel of her flesh against his. His fingers traced the line of her jaw, then outlined her soft lips. His movements stilled when her eyes fluttered open.

"Good morning," he breathed, his mouth lightly brushing hers. When he felt an answering response, he settled his lips firmly upon hers. She tasted like the ambrosia of Theams—rich, heady, devastating to the senses.

His hands cradled her head, moving it so he could gain better access to her sweet mouth. Like the caress of a light wind, his tongue slid along her lower lip, seeking entrance.

His deep-seated hunger for her exploded, shutting out all the reasons that he should not have her. His mouth devoured hers, while one hand slid down her neck beneath the ragged edge of her dress. He felt her stiffen at his action and pulled back.

Confusion, fear, and desire all mingled in her midnight-blue eyes. He drew in a deep breath and rolled away from her.

"Ladan?"

At the sound of her shaky voice, he sat up. "I'm sorry, Talia. I shouldn't have touched you." He stood and looked around the clearing. She held out his gloves and leather thong.

"I was sitting on them," she explained.

"But you knew what I was looking for, didn't you?" he asked, jerking on his gloves. "You read my thoughts, again."

"Yes."

The telepathic bond between them was strengthening. If he ever lay with her, he knew the bond between them would be unbreakable.

"Hurry and wash," he commanded as he tied the leather band around his head. "I will find us something to eat."

Talia watched him disappear into the thick foliage, grateful for a brief respite from his overwhelming presence. She scooted over to the edge of the pool and bathed her face. Her heart still pumped wildly from his closeness, and she felt giddy, out of control.

Pleasure. Is that what this trembling of her stomach was? Or perhaps the reaction Ladan evoked went beyond the mere physical. But how could she know, never having experienced anything like this before?

The feelings he invoked frightened her. Each time Ladan touched her it felt as if he were pulling her deeper and deeper into a black hole. And everyone knew nothing ever emerged from a black hole.

His presence behind her broke into her thoughts. She turned to him. Ladan frowned as he handed her a gar root, but remained quiet as they ate. It disturbed him that she could sense him near, and the longer they were together the stronger the vibrations became.

Ladan allowed her to walk for a brief time, but when she began to limp, he swept her into his arms and carried her. Talia made no protest, resting her head against his shoulder.

She must have slept because when she woke with a start, the jungle stood strangely silent. Talia peered up at Ladan.

"You feel it, too," Ladan whispered, his eyes scanning the path before them.

"Yes."

He gently set her down. "Something is wrong. Ready your laser," he commanded. Cautiously, he crept forward, his weapon in his hand.

Two men came crashing from the trees above, sending Ladan sprawling. Before Talia could raise her laser, she was seized from behind. The heavily muscled arm around her neck pressed down, cutting off her air while her attacker wrestled the gun from her grip.

"Get up, bounty hunter, and no tricks."

Talia watched in horror as one of the men kicked Ladan in the ribs. Slowly, Ladan rolled onto his back and stared up at his captor. The snarl that crossed Ladan's face made her jump against the imprisoning arm.

"Well, well, if it isn't the illustrious Captain Neils. Have you acquired a new fighter since the last time we met?"

The tall man flushed and kicked out again. Ladan caught his foot and twisted it, flinging the captain to the ground. Instantly, Ladan jumped on his back, capturing the struggling man's arm and pressing it high between his shoulder blades.

"Release the captain or the female dies."

Ladan looked at the man holding Talia. The violence churning in Ladan's golden eyes made the soldier step back and position Talia directly in front of him. Ladan released Neils's arm and stood. The third man instantly clamped Ladan's wrists into heavy metal manacles.

Captain Neils stood, brushing off his dark green uniform. Without warning, he backhanded Ladan across the jaw. Ladan tumbled to the ground.

Talia cried out and surged forward. Her captor cuffed her, then pushed her to the ground.

The commander eyed his two prisoners. "You have been a great deal of trouble to catch, Ladan. More trouble than you're worth, in my opinion, but Menoth wanted you caught and brought to him." He stroked his cheek as he studied Talia. "Where's the Geala?"

"Killed when we crashed on Alter," Ladan calmly answered.

Neils slowly circled Talia, studying her from several different angles. "She doesn't look Geala, but then why would any female travel with you of her own volition?" He lunged and grabbed Talia's left hand. She fought him, but her meager strength was no match for the powerful Dyne officer. Brutally, he pulled back the fingers of her left hand.

An evil grin split his lips when he saw the damning mark in Talia's palm. "So the Geala was killed?" Neils threw the question over his shoulder at Ladan. "It appears to me that you lie, bounty hunter. My orders are to kill the Geala, but after seeing her, I think Menoth would prefer we brought her to him."

"No!" Ladan roared, leaping to his feet. The other soldiers instantly grabbed him before he could fling himself at Neils.

Neils laughed, a dark sound that caused Talia to shiver. "Will it tear out your guts, Ladan, if I take the pretty little Geala and give her to your most hated enemy? Menoth's last wife was Geala. Perhaps he would

HUNTER'S HEART

like another—that is unless she has already taken a mate. Oh, well, it wouldn't matter to Menoth if she had a mate or not. He would like to use her either way."

Darkness pressed in on Talia. Neils caught her as she slumped.

Surprised, he glanced at Ladan. "It appears I frightened her." He shrugged, then slung Talia over his shoulder. "Take his knives from him," he commanded his men. Certain Ladan was disarmed, Neils started off to where their ship had landed.

As they marched through the jungle, Ladan decided that if he could not engineer their escape, he would slay Talia before he allowed her to fall into Menoth's hands. He would rather see her dead than have her suffer the hell his mother had endured.

By the time they reached the deserted jungle city where the Dyne ship landed, night had fallen. Because of the turbulent gases that gather above the surface during the hours of dark, they had to wait until the next morning to depart.

Ladan and Talia faced each other across the campfire. Captain Neils kept Talia at his side, carefully out of Ladan's reach.

As the three Dyne soldiers talked and ate, Talia carefully observed them. They were not as tall as Ladan, but their bodies were heavily muscled. They had the peculiar diamond-shaped pupils, but their eyes were green, not gold like Ladan's. Her eyes fell on Captain Neils's hands. The harsh scaling across their backs and across his forehead repelled her. Odd how the same trait in Ladan was not offensive to her.

The Dyne made no effort to restrain Talia, much to Ladan's surprise. If they were to escape, she would be the key. His poor tasha. He would again call on her to go against her father's teaching of peace and fight these soldiers. She had read his mind before. He counted on her doing so again.

Talia

She turned to him.

My laser is on the ground by the captain's feet.

Her eyes located the weapon.

Pick it up, little one, and hold it on the captain.

She glanced back at him for reassurance. He nodded in confirmation. Neils laughed at something one of the other men said. Her hand inched toward the weapon, expecting at any moment to be discovered. She flinched when she felt the cold handle of the laser. Grabbing the weapon, she stood, her knees shaking.

Captain Neils's head jerked up in surprise. "What do you plan to do with that laser?"

"Release him," she commanded. Her steady voice surprised her, and from the look on the Dyne's face, she surprised him, too.

Ladan stood and held out his hands to the soldier who had shackled him. The soldier waited for his captain's order. Talia fired a shot over the soldier's head to prod him. Her tactic worked.

As the right manacle fell free, Talia noticed a movement to her right. Without thought, she turned and fired her laser, killing the soldier before he could shoot her. Neils knocked the gun from her hand, then delivered a single blow to Talia's cheek. She collapsed at his feet.

Ladan exploded into action. He clutched the dangling handcuff and, with one powerful stroke, he hit the soldier in front of him. The single blow to his temple killed the Dyne. Before he could regain his balance, another body crashed into Ladan. Neils and Ladan rolled, their fists landing blows. When the thrashing bodies were finally still, Neils was on top.

Groggy from the blow, Talia groped for the gun. Instead her fingers closed around Ladan's knife, and she pulled it from its sheath. Knowing only that she had to save Ladan, she rose to her knees and buried the knife between Neils' shoulder blades. She watched in detached horror as the captain clawed his back in an effort to dislodge the weapon. Finally, he turned on her. He died clutching Talia's legs.

Talia stood frozen, staring at blood staining the captain's shirt.

"Talia, are you all right?" Ladan asked, rolling to his feet.

When she did not respond, Ladan instantly knew that the shock of her actions had set in. He guided her toward the campfire and settled her on a fallen log so that the carnage was out of her sight.

"Everything's fine, Talia. You're a brave warrior."

Her glassy-eyed expression worried him, but before he could reassure her, he needed to dispose of the soldiers' bodies. He jerked his knife from Neils' back, wiping off the blood on the captain's shirt, then heaved the man over his shoulder.

"Too bad it was Talia that killed you, you bastard. I would have loved to have had that honor myself," he muttered to the dead man. "Your death would have been more prolonged and painful if I had done it."

When he judged he was far enough from the camp so Talia would not run into the body, he pitched Neils into a bush. "I hope every carrion eater on this planet feasts on your worthless bones."

Quickly, he retrieved the other two bodies and threw them beside Neils. Just before he threw the last body on the pile, he searched the soldier's pockets for the key to his shackles. He wanted to remove the manacle hanging off his right wrist. It had been helpful in killing the Dyne, but he doubted that Talia, in her state, would find the bracelet reassuring.

Ladan cursed when his search turned up no key. Obviously, the man had dropped it when he'd been hit. Finding that key among the debris at night would be an impossible task. The thought did not improve his disposition.

When he returned to camp, Talia did not move or acknowledge him in any way. Instead, she stared blankly into the leaping flames of the fire.

"Little Geala," he crooned softly as he knelt before her. His arms slipped around her waist, drawing her close. Her stiff body told him that she was slipping away from him into a dark void from which she might never emerge. Madness was not uncommon among her kind.

How could he save her? How could he reach into her isolation and draw her out again?

Mating is different for a Geala than for a Dyne. His mother's words rang clearly through Ladan's mind. *It is a joining of the mind and soul as well as the physical.*

And does your mind join with father's?

Yes . . . and that is the hardest part of all, for I see into his mind and know the violence there.

Ladan gazed into Talia's sightless eyes. If he would called upon the mysterious bond that formed the first time a Geala mated would it save her? Could she draw enough stability from his thoughts, his feelings to counteract the horror and fear that were pulling her mind into the void?

But if he took her, then Talia would forever consider

him her mate. Was the price of her sanity too high to pay?

No, he argued to himself. To join with the tasha would hardly be a hardship. This physical joining was what his body had craved since the first instant he saw Talia. Now, at least, his lust could be cloaked in a noble gesture.

Quickly, he stripped off his gloves and cupped her face. Her skin was cold. "There is only one way I know to call you back from your darkness," he explained. Perhaps she could not hear him, but the voiced excuse eased his mind.

His mouth gently brushed over hers.

Nothing.

His right hand slipped down her neck. The dangling shackle clanked against its mate around his wrist. He jerked both hands away and stared at the offensive object, his thoughts trying to grasp at something deep in his subconscious.

Suddenly he knew how to unlock Talia's mind.

He took her left hand and tenderly placed a kiss in the middle of her palm. It wasn't enough for him. He had to have more. His tongue flicked out and caressed the blue star, laving it with hot moisture. His lips and tongue delighted in every square centimeter of her hand, doing the things he had fantasized about since the dust storm on Petar. Finally, when he could stand it no longer, he pressed his left palm to hers.

Hot, pulsing electricity shot through him.

Talia's eyes flickered.

Encouraged, he lowered his lips to hers, but never released his hold on her hand. There was a slight movement of her mouth, but nothing he could call a response.

"Talia, sweet child of the moon, come to me. Come

out of your darkness into the light. Reach out to me." He breathed his throaty plea between hot, drugging kisses. "Come to me, *my tenata*. Come."

His tongue plunged into her mouth, feasting on her sweetness. Soon his passion erased all rational thoughts from his consciousness. But instead of acting on his Dyne instinct of taking his gratification without any thought to the female, a new, unknown instinct emerged. This impulse took nothing from his fierce desire, but tempered his actions with gentleness. For the first time in his life, he wanted to give as much pleasure as he received.

He stripped, then tenderly removed Talia's clothes. Her body was no longer stiff but moved with the touch of his hands. Her warming skin was as smooth as liquid mercury, the color as rich as gold. With each stroke, each kiss, he felt as if he were melting, merging with the female in his arms. The driving need in him grew stronger, like a sudden madness over which he had no control.

He stretched out over her, marveling at how perfectly she fit him, as if the Creator had made them for each other. Pulling her hands above her head, he clasped her left hand in his. When he entered her, a shock ran through him, like the entire planet had just been hit by a huge meteor.

His eyes locked with Talia's and in that millisecond a bond formed. A bond that would last a lifetime.

When he began to move again, he felt the building energy storm. The heat was like plunging into a star, where the intense fire melded two separate elements into one. And then pleasure, as vast as the Andromeda galaxy which he called home, exploded in him, filling him with brilliant color and light. His hungry lips covered hers as she answered his cry. When he could breathe again he rolled to his side, taking Talia with him.

"You are mine now," he whispered into her tawny hair.

He pulled a black-and-gold band from his arm and placed it high on Talia's arm. The metal band that had only reached three-quarters of the way around his thick biceps slid down her small arm. With one hand he compressed the band to fit her.

His fingers raised her chin so he could look into her eyes. The indigo eyes were alert. Pushing her head down, he gruffly commanded, "Sleep. Tomorrow we will deal with the consequences of this night."

The shackles on his wrist rattled as he ran his hand over Talia's back. Holding up his hand, he watched the metal swing from his wrist. "I guess I'm not the only one now shackled."

Chapter 7

Ladan came instantly awake. Years of living on the razor's edge had taught him to come from a deep sleep into immediate alertness. He scanned the camp, making sure everything was secure before he allowed himself to look at the sleeping female in his arms.

He gazed tenderly down at her. How trustingly she curled into his body. Her lush curves and creamy complexion belied her Geala heritage.

Sometime during the night, her hair had unraveled from its braid, leaving her glorious mane to spill out around her head. Lightly, he smoothed several strands away from her cheek. He frowned as his fingers came into contact with the golden circlet on her forehead. In spite of everything that had happened, the circlet had not been lost or even disturbed. He longed to remove it, but he sensed if he did he would wake Talia.

Looking down at her, Ladan worried about her reaction once she left the oblivion of sleep. Although the deed was done and there was nothing he could do to change it, perhaps it would be better if she woke alone instead of naked in his arms. Carefully he moved away from her and slipped on his pants and boots. Walking to the Dyne fighter, he easily located the emergency food supply and removed several packets and a cooking bowl. He would fix Talia something hot to drink. As he was leaving, he spotted a dark green cloak thrown across the pilot's chair. He grabbed it, thinking it would make a perfect blanket for Talia.

After covering her to preserve her modesty and his sanity, he rebuilt the fire and boiled a packet of the fresh water he found on board. He added a generous amount of crushed ginter berries and allowed it to steep several minutes before pouring himself a cup. The drink, highly prized among his father's people, had a biting, acerbic flavor. It was one of the few things his mother had enjoyed on Darka.

He glanced at Talia. Would she like this tea? He took another large swallow of the hot liquid. The shackles on his wrist clanked. He growled a harsh oath, then rammed his foot into the dangling cuff, braced it against the ground, and pulled with all his strength. The chain snapped. Ladan looked ruefully at the remaining manacle. Well, at least he didn't have the other cuff banging around on his wrist.

"Would not it have been easier to unlock them?"

Ladan whirled at the sound of Talia's voice. She was sitting with the cloak wrapped around her. She appeared in control of herself. The only sign that things were not normal was the slight blush staining her cheeks.

"The key's missing. The guard must've dropped it when I hit him."

All the color fled from her face, and Ladan cursed himself for being a fool. He turned and poured her a cup of the tea.

"Drink this," he commanded, squatting before her. "It will soothe you."

Cupping her hands around the metal cup, Talia sipped the red liquid. Her lips puckered when she swallowed. Ladan grinned at her reaction.

"Take another sip. It takes several swallows before you are comfortable with the taste."

"What is it?"

"Ginter. Really it's crushed ginter berries. The bush grows on Darka. Tea from the berries has been consumed on Darka since recorded time. The drink is a stimulant."

By the fourth gulp, Talia could swallow without grimacing. In spite of the taste, the drink was refreshing.

"You need not study me with such a concerned frown, Ladan," she murmured between mouthfuls. "I will not shatter into a million pieces."

Ladan sat on the log next to her. "Talk to me, Talia. Tell me what you are feeling."

Her eyes met his. Doubts and pain clouded her blue eyes. Ladan gathered her close.

"It's all right, little Geala. You did only what had to be done."

"But I killed two men."

His fingers forced up her chin. "They would have taken you to Menoth, and that would have been a living death for you. If that does not satisfy your Geala conscience, then think of what would have happened to the Alliance if you had been captured."

"It was not myself or the Alliance I was thinking about. It was you. I could not allow them to harm you."

Ladan pulled her against him and kissed the top of her head. "Is that so bad?"

"No. You misunderstand. It was the ease with which I killed that disturbs me. I acted on instinct, yet I am sure my father never had such an impulse in his life."

"I'm sure you're right."

The cloak around Talia had slipped, and she noticed for the first time the black and gold band on her upper arm. Her eyes flew to Ladan's for an explanation.

"Among the Dyne a wife is marked by her husband. You now carry my brand. When we arrive at Ezion Geber, I will record the marriage. Declared marriages are legal as long as they are registered within a year of their inception."

A small frown creased her brow as she studied the intricately worked armband.

"I'm sorry, Talia. If there had been any other way, I would have taken it. I did not want to bind you to me."

"I understand. If not for you, I would still be lost in an endless void. Thank you, Ladan."

He breathed a sigh of relief. She was reacting to the situation better than he expected. After brushing a kiss across her lips, he stood. "Perhaps we should search for a spring or stream where you can wash while I prepare our former captors's fighter for flight."

"I would like that."

Ladan scooped up her clothes and handed them to her along with a laser. "You never can be too careful on this planet."

The deserted city was overgrown by jungle. Most of the buildings were only tumbled-down ruins with foliage growing between the cracks of the remaining stones. Off the main square Ladan found a small pool surrounded by a partial floor that probably was once a bathhouse.

He handed Talia a yellow bar of soap he had pilfered from the ship. "Don't take long," he cautioned before leaving her to her bath.

Talia dropped the cloak and stepped into the warm water. She sighed, grateful that Alter 3 had numerous geothermal springs for her body ached in the most unusual spots. She blushed, knowing the cause.

She could not recall with clarity the entire chain of events from the previous night. She remembered staring down at Captain Neils's back, seeing the spreading stain on his shirt, and then blackness had descended. It had been Ladan's voice floating through the mists, like a life line, that she had grasped.

My tenata.

Fire had touched her hand, racing along all her nerve endings, collecting in her loins. The one thing she distinctly remembered was the instant the bond between her and Ladan had formed. It was as if he had taken her inside him, and the ensuing explosion created a new and different person. A person now complete.

She wished she could clearly recall each detail and feeling of the encounter, then blushed at her wantonness. Surely, such thoughts were wrong. Her father would never approve of her shameless desires. And, yet, Talia found a part of her wanted to repeat the experience. Married couples mated more than once, didn't they? They must, or how else did a female conceive? And if a couple must mate to conceive, then didn't it stand to reason her father must have touched her mother in the same way Ladan had her?

Her halves were at war again, her desires conflicting

with her values. To touch was to show disrespect, and yet touching Ladan brought a host of wonderful feelings.

She threw back her head and searched the sky. "Who am I? I kill without thought. I derive satisfaction in ways I know are unacceptable. Each day brings more that I do not understand. Oh, Creator, help me."

A single tear trickled down her cheek. "I am lost and do not know my way back."

"Talia."

Ladan's voice startled her out of her despondency. Quickly, she wiped away the tear, but Ladan, standing at the edge of the broken floor, saw her actions. He knelt on one knee and cupped her face.

"You had no choice, Talia. I took that decision away from you. I am your mate."

She tried to smile, but her lower lip trembled. She watched in amazement as his eyes darkened with desire. His head dipped, but he stopped himself a breath away from her. Jerking away, he stood.

"Hurry and dress," he commanded, turning away.

A sharp stab of disappointment pricked her. She had wanted that kiss. Confused and disturbed at her own wayward thoughts, Talia hurriedly dressed in her tattered coat-dress and pants.

As they neared the camp, Talia spotted a shiny object among the tall grass. She stopped and picked it up.

"I believe you were looking for this." In her outstretched hand rested the key to his shackle.

Raising his wrist, he asked, "Would you do the honors?"

"My pleasure."

The springing of the lock echoed in the quiet clearing.

"I wish I could release you as easily," he gently told her, rubbing his wrist.

Talia's lips tightened. Was she so lacking as a female that he wished he was not her mate? Or was there another reason? And why did he feel guilty for saving her sanity? She tried to read his mind, but for some odd reason, his thoughts were closed to her.

"Let's eat. Then I will see if I can fly the Dyne fighter."

Talia tried the meat from the packet Ladan handed her. The white color and strong taste repulsed her. She returned the pouch.

"I think I prefer daffus fruit."

"I'm not surprised. Mother did not care for ketn meat, either."

Talia poured herself another cup of ginter. She stared into the red liquid, trying to think of the best way to frame her question.

"Ladan, what does *my tenata* mean?"

Under the deep bronze of his skin, Ladan's cheeks colored. His reaction surprised her. "It's a Darkan endearment."

"I guessed as much. But what does it mean?"

Ladan's body stiffened. Clearly, he did not wish to answer her question. She had given up hope he would answer when he murmured, "Heart of my heart."

He threw away the food pouch and stood. Anger radiated from him like heat from a fire. Yet, oddly enough, that anger was not directed at her but at himself. The use of the endearment had shamed him.

Towering over her, fully dressed in his vest and crossing belts, he was an intimidating sight. She swallowed nervously, not knowing what to expect next. Ladan turned and walked to the ship. When he disappeared through the hatch, Talia jumped to her feet and followed.

The instant she crossed the threshold Talia's senses cried out a warning. "Ladan, all is not right."

"I see nothing wrong," Ladan answered, scanning the control panel. He pressed the button to activate the computer.

"Voice identification," the computer's voice responded.

Ladan looked above the windshield and spotted the small, red blinking light. "Damn the bastard." Whirling, he grabbed Talia's wrist and ran out the door.

"Ladan, what's wrong?" she gasped.

He didn't answer but raced toward a large stone wall on the far side of the city. They had just reached the shelter when an explosion ripped through the air. The shock knocked both of them off their feet. Quickly, Ladan covered her body with his to protect her from the flaming debris.

When he felt it was safe, Ladan peered over the wall at the burning ship.

"What happened?" Talia asked, glancing over the wall.

"Neils had a voice lock on the ship. If anyone else but him tried to activate the computer, it would trip a delay mechanism that would blow the ship after a minute."

"How did you know that?"

"I knew what Neils had done when the computer asked for a voice identification. It's a common practice to insure against your vessel being stolen. If I had been more alert, I would have noticed that light above the windshield. That bulb is a dead giveaway the ship is rigged, rather like a warning."

Ladan stared at the burning remains of the vessel and shook his head. "I guess we walk to Nova Seth after all."

The jungle seemed to vibrate with Ladan's frustrated desire. The hardest thing he'd ever done was turn away from Talia this morning. What he had wanted more than anything was to take her in his arms and show her all the delights of passion. But it was too soon for her. She had barely recovered from the shock of killing the Dyne soldiers, and he knew her emotions were still too unstable to withstand his driving ardor.

With savage blows of his knife, Ladan slashed away the vine blocking his path. What he felt for Talia surpassed simple lust. That had been proven hours ago when he put her needs above his. Never had that happened before. She was turning him inside out, dredging up things in him that he never guessed existed, and generally ruining his well-defined existence.

He grabbed the leafy plant in his way and ripped it out of the ground by its roots. He didn't need or want these frivolous emotions that Talia stirred. They would only distract him from his mission of getting her safely to Ezion Geber. Yet, if he were honest with himself, he had to admit the feelings she stirred were anything but frivolous.

When he had made love to her, the Geala bond had formed for Talia, making him her mate. He expected that. What he hadn't expected was that the bond had finally formed for him, too. When his eyes had met hers, something was triggered deep inside him. Odd, that after all the females he had bedded, suddenly this Geala bond had sprung to life. But, then again, there were several previous unknown traits that had appeared since he'd known Talia.

These odd feelings are simply a result of unfulfilled desire, he sternly told himself. He wanted the female so much it was warping his mind.

For once, Talia welcomed the sapping heat of Alter 3 and the endless jungle they had to struggle through. Fighting the elements kept her mind off the events of the previous day.

Ladan was strangely remote as he fought his way through the foliage. She sensed his agitation but could not determined its source. His mind remained closed to her.

She ran her fingers over the armband. *Accept what has happened,* she told herself. *Nothing can be undone. Think of the future, of what will happen when you arrive at Ezion Geber.*

And, yet, even as she battled against the vision, scenes of the Dyne soldiers's violent deaths flashed through her mind. A whimper escaped her lips.

"Talia." Ladan grasped her arms and looked deep into her eyes. "It's time to stop. Rest here while I find us something to eat." He disappeared into the trees.

She didn't want to be alone with her memories. She wished her little catwig was here so she could laugh at its antics. But when the Dyne had overpowered them, the animal had been tossed into the jungle and fled.

Suddenly the darkness, heat, and silence pressed in on her, robbing her of breath. She stumbled to a log and sat down.

Fight the fear, Talia. Father would be ashamed if you gave in to the trembling.

She took a deep steadying breath and began to softly sing a lullaby.

> "Above the stars twinkle
> So bright and fine and free
> And among the stars that twinkle
> You will find a part of me."

Ladan stopped mid-stride when he heard the golden voice. He closed his eyes and listened. Something about the song disturbed him. It was as if he had heard it before, and yet where would he have heard such an innocent child's song in the hellish places where he had lived?

He shook off the silly mood and pushed his way through the bushes. The sight of Talia huddled on the log, hugging her knees, rocking back and forth ripped through his heart. When her eyes met his, he felt her joy at his return. It took the edge off his anger.

Handing her the fruit, he watched with amusement as she warily eyed the dead kelser hanging over his shoulder.

"You may not like meat, but I do. It's quite tasty when roasted over an open fire."

She doubtfully eyed the reptile.

After gathering enough wood and dead leaves, he started a small fire. He would smother the flames when he finished. He questioned the wisdom of building even a small blaze, for he did not want to alert anyone they were here, but he was in no mood to be cautious. He wanted meat, and he'd have it, consequences be damned!

They remained silent while the meat cooked. Ladan

sliced a piece of the roasted flesh and offered it to Talia. Hesitantly, she accepted it and took a bite. He could tell from her grimace that his tasha would never be a meat-eater.

"Would you like another piece?" The laughter in his eyes told her that he was teasing.

"I think not."

Ladan leaned close. "You're predictable."

"What do you mean?"

"Gealas don't like meat."

"Oh."

"What was that song I heard you singing earlier?"

Her faced colored. "A lullaby."

"One your mother sang to you?"

"No. My father taught me the song."

"Your father?"

Talia picked a leaf off the ground and began to shred it. "I know it sounds strange that Father would sing to me. He told me it was a common song taught to all children."

"No, Talia. It's not." What Talia had just said puzzled him. Why would a man who was logical, polite, emotionless, sing to his daughter?

His hands framed her face. Purple shadows circled her eyes, and the strain of the last days showed on her features. "You need to rest. Go and take care of your needs."

When she returned from the surrounding foliage, the fire had been extinguished and Ladan sat with his back against a fallen limb. He held out an arm and she settled beside him. She did not question the arrangement, nor was she uncomfortable with it. He was the only thing that stood between her and her nightmares.

* * *

Talia's whimper woke Ladan. He sensed she was reliving in her dreams the deaths of the Dyne soldiers. Tenderly, he stroked her cheek. "Talia, wake up." He had not put his gloves back on and the feel of her silky flesh against the sensitized skin of the blue star in his left palm sent stinging needles of pleasure through his body.

Her eyes flew open, and he clearly saw her panic. With a cry, she threw her arms around his neck.

"Ladan, will the terror never cease?"

He wrapped his arms around her waist and drew her flush against his body. His lips grazed her cheek. "Give yourself time, Talia. The wound will heal."

He was warmth and safety, driving away the demons of the night, giving her comfort for terror.

Ladan felt the fear drain out of her body only to be replaced by a different kind of tension. Tilting her chin up, he asked, "What do you remember of our joining?"

Gulping, she opened her mouth, then closed it. She tried again. "After stabbing the captain, I remember being alone in a suffocating darkness. Then I heard your voice. It led me out."

"What else?"

Talia felt the roots of her hair go red with embarrassment. "Your eyes . . . and fire."

Ladan's breath caught in his throat. The most expert seductress did not even have a tenth of the effect on him that Talia did. Unable to stop himself, Ladan's head swooped down, and he covered her mouth with his.

This night her responses were true, not dulled by terror. He pulled back to look into her eyes.

"I want you, Talia. As a male wants his mate."

His expression, dark with desire, caused a shiver to run down her spine. "I know."

"And that doesn't frighten you?"

"A little."

Every instinct he possessed screamed that she held her real motives in check. "What aren't you telling me?"

"I am curious." She placed her left hand on his chest.

He nearly convulsed from the pleasure-pain of her action. The heat of her blue star where it touched his chest branded him. Her non-Geala half was in control.

"I find myself wondering . . . about how . . . I wish I could have been fully aware of my reactions last night," she throatily admitted.

Ladan gaped at her in stunned surprise, then broke into laughter. "Little Geala, you shouldn't be so honest. It will get you in trouble."

She hung her head. "I know."

His hand covered hers and pressed it hard against his chest. "Do you feel the thudding of my heart?" His other hand settled between her breasts. "Yours is beating as hard as mine."

He smiled the knowing smile of a teacher about to impart a particularly wonderful lesson. "Tonight we will share the light." His lips covered hers with a hungry insistence, giving in to the desire that seemed always to rage just beneath the surface.

His kisses grew wild, and she had no control over her answering responses. He drew from her feelings and actions she never knew existed. He was a raging fire storm, burning up all her false actions, leaving only the true being.

The ending explosion of beauty caught her by surprise. When her breathing became normal, she peeked up at Ladan. His eyes were closed, his expression peaceful. She rubbed her cheek on his chest.

"Now I understand," she murmured.

"Understand what?" Ladan asked.

She jumped, surprised she had spoken the words out loud.

Ladan's eyes met hers. "What do you understand?"

She didn't want to answer, but from his expression she knew he would not let the comment pass. "What you meant when you told me of the pleasures of the flesh."

He grinned. "Wondrous, aren't they?"

Talia blushed.

"Go to sleep, little Geala, before I demonstrate more of those pleasures."

She rested her head on his chest. Her reaction to their lovemaking was shocking and unnerving. And she had no explanation for her behavior. Yet deep inside she knew two basic truths.

Ladan was her destiny.

Ladan was her mate.

Chapter 8

Nova Seth was a noisy, bustling city carved from the surrounding jungle. One moment they had been plowing through the dense foliage and the next standing at the edge of the city.

Looking at the towering buildings and busy streets, Talia stepped closer to Ladan and slipped her hand in his.

With a puzzled frown, he looked at her. "What's wrong?"

"I am frightened. This is an evil place."

Cupping her face, Ladan tenderly smiled. "Don't worry, Talia. I'll protect you."

She wanted to argue with him. Tell him it was more than just the evilness of the city that alarmed her. Like a suffocating shroud, darkness enveloped this place so tightly she doubted even Ladan could circumvent it. Instead, she squeezed his hand.

He gave her a chaste kiss on the forehead, then reached inside his vest and pulled out his gloves.

"Why are you putting those on?"

"Only you, Talia, know my true parentage. Until I deliver you safely to Ezion Geber I need to keep my secrets."

Grabbing her hand, he started into the city. "Don't let go."

He skirted the main square and the bazaar, working his way around the outside of the city to the vessel launch. Jeiel's vessel was not parked there, and Ladan did not like the looks of either of the men who were willing to take on passengers. He decided to give Jeiel one star day to show up. After that, he'd look for another way off Alter.

Standing outside the launch's electric gates, Ladan wondered where he was going to keep Talia for the next 27 star hours. He simply couldn't wander the city with her in tow. She needed food, shelter, and something decent to wear. There was no one on Alter 3 he trusted, but he knew of a tavern that was clean, where the patrons were not cheated. He had stayed at Zadok's inn when he was on Alter 3 before. He'd take Talia there.

As they walked down the street, Talia became painfully aware of her abbreviated outfit. In the damp heat of the jungle, exposing her limbs had been necessary, and she'd taken comfort from that fact. But now with all these males staring at her as if she was a piece of fruit they wished to consume, Talia felt degraded and ashamed.

Ladan noticed the salivating stares and glared at anyone who dared to take a second look at Talia. He glanced over his shoulder at her. From the dull stain of her cheeks and the low position of her head, he knew she was shamed by her appearance.

He wove his way through the tangled streets to an open bazaar where food and clothing merchants had set up stalls.

Passing by several clothing stalls, Ladan stopped in front of a small booth that displayed female apparel. "I wish to clothe this female from the skin out," he told the merchant.

The woman critically eyed Talia, then began to pull garments from the tables around the stall. Out of the corner of his eye, Ladan watched in amusement Talia's reaction to the handsome, black-skinned female.

"To what race does she belong?" Talia whispered in Ladan's ear.

"She is Cetus." Ladan turned her and pointed to the stall two booths away. "The green man over there is from Trifid."

"But Trifid is part of the Dyne Union."

"You forget, Talia, that Alter 3 is beyond the law of the Alliance. If you have the price, you can live on Alter."

"Your purchases, sir," the merchant said, handing Ladan a bundle. He dug into the belt crossing his chest and handed the woman a coin.

"A gold coin. I don't often receive one of these. Thank you, sir. And I hope your female enjoys the clothes."

The merchant's statement puzzled Talia. "What did the Cetus woman mean about the coin?"

"Within the Alliance, even among the members of the Dyne Union, credits are used as the medium of exchange. But here on Alter 3 and other renegade planets where people want anonymity and do not want their names fed into a computer, coins of silver, gold, platinum and jewels are used as currency. You are familiar with the concept of currency, aren't you?"

Her eyebrows raised. "Of course," she countered in an indignant tone. "Father and I bartered for the goods Lee brought us, but I have studied currency theories."

Ladan grinned. "Come along. I know a place where you can change."

The city was honeycombed with inns and taverns, ranging from those with dirt floors and raw wood furniture where the poor thieves gathered, to the expensive marbled-floor inns that catered to the wealthy aristocrats who came to buy the outlawed goods of Alter 3.

Ladan pulled Talia along the street, down several back alleys to a two-story stone building in one of the better sections of the city. Cautiously, he pushed open the door.

"May I help you?" asked the short, wiry man behind the long bar.

Before Ladan could respond, a large man at a nearby table stood. He was dressed in baggy pants and a loose white shirt.

"Ladan, you old dog, what are you doing here?" the handsome man asked as he shook the bounty hunter's hand.

"I'm here on business, Zadok, and need a room."

Zadok led them through the long taproom, past the scattered tables where men sat drinking, to a stairwell at the back of the building. After climbing the steps, Zadok opened the first door. The contrast from the drab hall to the rich appointments of the room awed Talia. The floor was covered with a thick patterned rug, the walls draped in layers of gauzy fabric. In the center of the room sat a low table surrounded by mounds of brightly-colored cushions.

Talia felt Zadok's eyes on her as she sat next to Ladan. She wanted to squirm under the scrutiny, but decided that would be cowardly.

"Who is the female with you, my friend?"

Zadok's lazy tone did not fool Ladan. Zadok was no fool, and Ladan knew he would have to be careful with what he said. "Talia is my mate."

Eyes wide, Zadok snapped upright from his reclining position. "You are teasing, of course."

Pointing to Talia's armband, he replied, "No. The band marks her as mine."

Zadok studied both Ladan and the female. "What do you wish from me?" he queried.

"I have many enemies in this city. I wish a safe haven for Talia while I arrange for a ship to fly us out of here."

Zadok poured a golden liquid into three silver cups and handed them to his guests. "There have been rumors that the Dyne have marked you for death."

"That's nothing new."

"But it's said that you have bound yourself to a quest to bring a Geala to Ezion Geber to save the Alliance."

With effort, Ladan leashed the flaring anger racing through his veins. He would find the person who betrayed him and rip his head from his body and hang it from the gates of Ezion Geber. "You know the Dyne will go to any lengths to dispose of me."

Zadok shrugged. "I only sought to warn you."

Ladan nodded. "Talia needs water for a bath and something to eat. I will warn you she is not a meateater," he added, standing.

Talia was shown to a small chamber. The furnishing paled beside Zadok's, but Talia welcomed the simple bed with clean sheets, table and chairs. But what she really loved was the attached bathing room.

Ladan showed her how to work the faucets. "While you bathe, I want to go back to the vessel launch and see if Jeiel has landed." He took her by the shoulders. "Don't open the door to anyone. Do you understand?"

"What about you?"

"I have the key. Talia, although Zadok has never betrayed me, there have been rumors his allegiance can be bought."

"Perhaps I should go with you."

"No. That would put you at greater risk. We'll have to trust Zadok, but we'll not stay here long enough for his loyalties to change." He tenderly kissed her left palm. "Go, enjoy your bath."

At the door, he was met by a servant holding a tray. His stomach growled, but he had no time to stop and eat. He grabbed a chunk of bread and cheese, then locked the door after the servant departed. Quickly he found his way back to the vessel launch.

He had just walked through the electric gates when he spotted Jeiel's disk-shaped craft. Breathing a sigh of relief that something finally had gone right, Ladan rushed across the yard.

"Jeiel," he called, entering the open hatch.

A tall, well-muscled man with long brown hair and piercing green eyes stepped into view. Ladan paused when he saw the laser in Jeiel's hand.

"Do you have a complaint against me?" Ladan calmly asked.

A wide smile broke across Jeiel's face. "Nope. I just can't be sure who will wander onto my ship in this hellhole of the star system." He slipped the laser into

HUNTER'S HEART   109

the holster hanging at his hip. "Why did you decide to crash your vessel on this piece of trash?"

Ladan grabbed Jeiel's wrist in a sign of greeting, ignoring Jeiel's chastening. Jeiel was the only man Ladan would trust to guard his back. The two had met in a bar on Sor. Ladan had a prisoner shackled to his wrist when the prisoner's five brothers found them. Jeiel hadn't like the odds, so he entered the fray and prevented Ladan from being skewered on the point of a two-edged anlace, taking the dagger himself. The wound would had been insignificant to Jeiel, but Ladan viewed the incident differently. He would give his life for Jeiel.

"I had no choice. The Dyne attacked my ship. I barely made it here."

Jeiel rubbed the back of his neck. "Yeah, I heard the Dyne had put a price on your head. What happened to the Geala?"

The softening that crept across Ladan's face startled Jeiel. Never, *never* had he seen such an expression of tenderness on the mysterious bounty hunter's face.

"She's waiting for me at Zadok's tavern."

"She?" Jeiel sounded as if someone had kicked him in the seat of the pants.

"Yes, the Geala's female. She's also a tasha."

Jeiel shook his head. "I don't understand."

Quickly, Ladan explained his and Talia's odyssey from Petar to Alter 3. "Even after we crashed, the Dyne still knew we were alive and sent soldiers. That's why I need you to fly us out of this city as soon as possible."

"I'm ready to leave now."

"I'll go get Talia." At the door Ladan paused. "You should know Talia is my mate."

Jeiel stared at the empty hatch. If Alter's sun suddenly went supernova, he could not have been more surprised.

Ladan, the loner, the most notorious bounty hunter in the star system, had taken a mate. A tasha. Better yet, a tasha who was part Geala.

Jeiel shook his head. Ladan married to a stiff-necked, formal female who was half Geala by birth but probably all Geala in manner. Why, the idea was positively ludicrous. Ladan always preferred—at least from the times he was with him—dark, passionate, full-bodied women whose idea of commitment was staying with a man until they were paid for their services.

So why, suddenly, had Ladan married? Opposites attract. A positive charge was always drawn to a negative one. Perhaps the basic law of physics held true for higher beings. He shrugged his shoulders. Perhaps.

Jeiel turned to the main control panel of his ship and began his preflight check. He was anxious to meet this tasha that had married Ladan.

The soap and hot water restored Talia's flagging spirits. After drying herself on the large soft towel, she moved to the bed where her clothes were laid out. The only undergarment the merchant had included was a little blue scrap of material she guessed was suppose to pass as underpants. Next, she slipped on the blue floor-length dress. The sleeves were loose, ending at her wrists. A belt, a darker shade than her dress, was included.

Talia looked into the mirror. The deep vee of the neckline showed too much skin for her taste, and the light fabric molded faithfully to her curves. She would have preferred her own clothes, yet they were in such poor condition that there was no other alternative.

After plaiting her hair, she enjoyed the meal left on

the table. Another pitcher of the golden liquid they'd shared with Zadok had been delivered with the meal. After finishing two goblets, she crawled onto the bed and went to sleep.

An uneasy feeling crept up Zadok's neck. He looked around the market, seeking the source of his apprehension but found nothing unusual or out of place. He strolled to the stall where cheap jewelry was sold.

"Good afternoon, Clay."

"Zadok." The tall black man with golden eyes moved to the front of his booth.

Picking up a necklace of silver and stone, Zadok asked, "How is business today?" He glanced up, waiting for the other man's coded reply.

"Slow. Do you like lapis lazuli stone in that necklace?"

Zadok's eyes narrowed. When Clay used the stone's full name, it signaled an alert. Zadok moved to the side of the stall and handed Clay the necklace. "What have you seen?" Zadok asked, his voice a mere whisper.

"Dyne soldiers at the edge of the square. And I thought I saw one of your employees with them."

A low curse slipped from Zadok's mouth. "Did you recognize which one?"

"No."

With a nod, Zadok turned and hurried back to his tavern, a feeling of dread in the pit of his stomach. He swore on Melinda's grave that he would avenge her death and that was why he'd chosen the life he had. To live on Alter 3 wouldn't have been his choice, but that's where he was needed and where he willingly went. As he raced down the street, he prayed he would be in time to save this female.

* * *

The pounding on the door woke Talia.

"I've come for the tray," a man called. "Let me in."

It took a moment for Talia's reeling senses to settle. "Please, come back later."

"I need the tray now," came the growled response.

She wanted to help the servant, but Ladan had been very explicit about not opening the door. The last time she disobeyed him the consequences had been dire. She would not disobey him again.

Climbing off the bed, she went to the door. "I am sorry, but I cannot open the door."

She heard the murmur of voices. And then, "Just break down the damn door."

She jumped back just as the door crashed in. Talia's heart raced when she saw the two Dyne soldiers. They were accompanied by the little man who had tended the bar downstairs.

"Hurry," he said, "before Zadok discovers what I've done."

Talia looked around the room for the laser Ladan had left her. She spotted it on the table by the tray. As she lunged, the Dyne soldier stepped in front of her, blocking her path.

Some primitive instinct seized her, and she began to fight like a crazed animal, kicking, scratching and biting her captor. She couldn't be taken. She couldn't be separated from Ladan.

"Are you sure this female is a Geala?" the second soldier asked, watching Talia fight.

"She was with the bounty hunter. Look at her hand if you have any doubt."

HUNTER'S HEART

The little man's words exploded in Talia's head, and she screamed. "No! Let go of me!"

One of the Dyne grabbed her left wrist and squeezed until Talia's knees buckled and her hand opened.

"See," the wiry man crowed. "There's the mark."

The soldier holding Talia grunted and pulled a pair of cuffs out of his belt and locked them around Talia's wrists. Yanking her to her feet, he pushed her toward the door.

Ladan! she cried silently.

Suddenly the doorway was filled with Zadok's imposing figure. In his hand he held a nerve gun, which halted an enemy with a wave of pain. "I see you have decided to branch out on your own, Marc."

The bartender moved closer to the Dyne soldiers. "The reward was too high to ignore."

Zadok shook his head. "That's too bad. You were a decent bartender." He aimed and fired. Marc fell to the floor with a howl, writhing in pain. Before either soldier could move, Zadok shot them also.

Talia wanted to cover her ears with her hands to shut out the agonizing cries, but her shackles prevented it. She closed her eyes.

Ladan.

Gentle hands on her shoulders caused her eyes to fly open.

Zadok smiled at her. "Come away from here until I can locate Ladan and send for him."

"That will not be necessary," Talia told him. "He is below and on his way up here now."

Before Zadok could respond, Ladan's voice echoed down the hall. "Talia!"

She stepped into the hall and immediately was swallowed in Ladan's strong embrace. He nudged her head up and covered her lips with his.

Zadok cleared his throat. "Perhaps it would be best to finish this another time." He handed Ladan the key to the handcuffs.

Talia held up her wrists. "It appears you and I share an ability to get ourselves shackled."

"It appears so," he agreed, releasing her.

Ladan glanced into the room at the three moaning men, then back at Zadok.

"Marc was the one who brought them."

"Then I'll kill him," Ladan calmly stated.

"I'll do that, as well as dispose of the Dyne soldiers."

"Why? Why would you do that for me?"

"Because there was another young female a long time ago that I couldn't save. Besides, I did not wish to make you my enemy. Oh, and tell Joakim I'm well."

"Joakim?"

"There are many of us who work for him."

A knowing look passed between the two men. Ladan shook Zadok's hand, then turned to go.

"Wait," Talia cried.

"What is it?"

She lifted up her skirt to show him her bare toes. "I need my shoes and the laser."

His eyebrow shot up in surprise. His little Geala remembering the laser? Did that mean he was corrupting her at light-speed, or was she learning how to take care of herself?

Before he could respond, she dashed into the room. He watched as she paused by Zadok's side and heard her murmur 'thank you'. In the next moment she stood by him, slipping on her battered leather shoes. He should've bought her another pair this afternoon.

Silently, he moved down the hall to the stairs, watchful for any further trouble. He paused at the back door, surveying the dark alley. Earlier, when he felt Talia calling to him as he approached the tavern, his heart nearly stopped beating. Now that he knew the Dyne were aware of Talia's location, he needed to be twice as careful.

After assuring himself that the alley was clear, he pulled Talia out into the night. Her complete trust in him still made him uneasy, but oddly enough, he valued that trust.

They kept to the alleys, hugging the buildings as they made their way through the heart of the city. They were less than 200 meters from the gates of the launch area when Ladan hesitated.

"Ladan," Talia whispered.

"Yes, I feel the danger."

Four shabby men materialized from between two buildings, surrounding them.

Ladan breathed a sigh of relief when he saw the males were not Dyne soldiers but just some of the rabble that inhabited Alter 3.

"Surrender the female and we'll let you go," the tallest of the assailants instructed.

The smile Ladan gave the man chilled the warm night air. "No."

All of Talia's telepathic senses cried out in warning. Her hand slipped to the laser at her waist as she stepped closer to Ladan.

The leader quietly studied Talia. "Perhaps you would be willing to sell the female. I'll offer you 100 silver coins."

Talia shuddered as she felt the pulsating violence radiating out of Ladan. He was ready to kill.

"I doubt you have two silver coins to your name," Ladan calmly replied. "But it doesn't matter. The female is not for sale at any price."

Bowing, the man said, "As you wish." He looked at the three men behind Talia and Ladan, giving them a quick nod. A thick metal bar appeared in one of the assailant's hands and he swung it, hitting Ladan in the temple. Ladan staggered and fell to his knees, holding his head. All three men descended on him, kicking and punching.

Ladan grabbed the knife in his belt and plunged it into the stomach of one of the men. He cut a second man across the forearm and was about to bury his knife in the man's chest, when the third man caught the side of his head with the metal bar. Ladan went down.

In the mass of writhing bodies, it was impossible for Talia to get a clear shot at the attackers. Her attention diverted, she failed to notice the leader creep up on her.

"Ladan!" Talia screamed.

The man lunged, grasping her around the waist and clamping his hand across her mouth.

"Shut up or I'll break your neck," he hissed in her ear. When she continued to struggle, he released her, spun her about and hit her in the jaw. He caught her before she hit the ground.

"Ebes, why'd you do that?" one of the brutes demanded.

"Because I needed to shut her up."

"But you could've damaged the merchandise."

Cold eyes speared the brute. "Do you question my expertise?"

"N-no."

"Good, because I wouldn't want to have to replace you." Ebes looked down at the female in his arms. In the five years he had been hunting females for Selmet to sell, he'd never come across such a delicate, beautiful female. The moment he had seen her in the bazaar this afternoon, he knew he would have to acquire her for Selmet. "Haef, the little love tap that I gave this one will give no permanent marks."

"What of the male?" Haef asked.

Glancing down at the still man, the leader grinned. "Leave him. No one will be shocked at a body in the alley."

With that, he headed toward Selmet's marble auction house. With the fortune he'd make from this sale, he could go into business for himself.

Chapter 9

Ladan staggered out of the alley into Jeiel's waiting arms. Worried that Ladan had not returned, Jeiel had gone looking for his friend.

"What happened?" Jeiel asked as he slipped his arm around Ladan's waist.

"Ambushed," he gasped, holding his throbbing side.

Jeiel tried to steer Ladan toward his ship, but he resisted.

"No. I must find Talia. They've taken her."

"Who, Ladan? Who attacked you?"

"Slavers."

The words made Jeiel pause. He knew that if they didn't find Talia in the next few hours, they would not find her at all. "Come back to my ship, Ladan, and let me tend your wounds. We can devise a plan to find her."

Ladan shook his head. "No, I want to start searching now."

Knowing how stubborn his friend was, Jeiel yielded to the inevitable. "All right, we'll do it your way, but come back with me to the ship so I can get another weapon before we go hunting."

Taking Ladan's grunt as an acceptance, Jeiel helped Ladan to his ship. After settling him in the pilot's chair, Jeiel poured a glass of Mythinan brandy and handed it to Ladan. "Drink this."

The burning liquid helped clear Ladan's senses. "Are there any auctions tonight or tomorrow?" he asked, watching Jeiel pull a stun gun and laser from the paneled compartment at the back of the cockpit.

"How would I know?" Jeiel responded.

"You have ways."

Jeiel shrugged.

"Zadok would know," Ladan said. He ignored the piercing pain in his side as he stood and walked to the open hatch.

In spite of his injuries, Ladan crossed the city in record time. All aches and pains he pushed from his mind, concentrating instead on how he would tear apart the bastards who had taken Talia from him. None would be alive tomorrow.

"Zadok," Ladan bellowed as he strode into the inn. He hoped that Zadok was finished disposing of Marc and the Dyne soldiers. From the back of the tavern came a muted noise. Ladan moved in that direction.

Zadok looked up from the sheet-covered body. "Ladan." He dropped the corpse's feet. "What are you doing here?"

"Some miscreants set upon us just before we reached the vessel launch and took Talia."

"Dyne?"

"No. Slavers. I came back to find out which acquisition houses have scheduled auctions tonight."

His eyes narrowed, Zadok rubbed his chin. "Selmet and Gosha."

"Will you lead us there?"

"Of course, but I need your help with this body."

Ladan pulled up the corner of the sheet and grunted in satisfaction. "Was Marc's death painful?"

"Tokia poison is always painful."

"Good. I just wished I could've administered the dose. Where do you want to dump this trash?"

"There is a body disposal plant at the end of the street. Gosha's house is not more than three blocks beyond that."

"Let's go."

Ebes carefully laid the female on the bed and stepped back to allow Selmet to examine her.

"Is she not everything I said she was?" Ebes asked.

Selmet remained quiet as he pulled Talia's dress up to her waist to inspect her legs. He pushed back her left sleeve, checking for possible defects. He turned to Ebes. "She'll do."

"I want fifty percent of the sale price for this one, Selmet."

The older man paused by the door. "That's a steep price."

"She's worth it."

"What makes you think I will pay you that much?"

"Because the Zicri ambassador is out in the auction room, and we all know what a passion the Zicri have for fair females. She's far beyond any other female we've had. She'll bring a high price."

Selmet nodded. "After this I'll tolerate no more gouging." He left the room.

"After this," Ebes murmured to the closed door, "I'll no longer need you, you old fool."

A black rage consumed Ladan as he walked to the body disposal with the corpse slung over his shoulder. He could never remember being this enraged, ready to decimate anything or anyone that stood between him and Talia.

They had taken what was his. They'd taken his mate. The thought of another male touching her, knowing the sweet taste of her love, was unbearable. He'd learned his father's lessons too well to accept anything less than the forfeit of the offenders' lives.

"Ladan, we're here." Zadok pointed out the chute where the body was to be thrown. After tossing the corpse into the opening, Ladan followed Zadok down the street.

Beyond his anger at the perpetrators, Ladan worried about the effect the kidnaping would have on Talia. She had been through so much in the last few days. How much more could she bear before her sanity snapped?

Then, with a blinding flash of insight, the truth hit Ladan. Although she was half Geala, Talia was not as brittle as a full-blooded Geala. There was a resiliency to her that he could only attribute to her unknown half. The experiences she had undergone would have broken a true Geala, driven them mad. Talia had only been bruised but not broken.

No matter what happened, his lovely moon child would survive.

"Ladan, we're here at the house of Gosha." Zadok waited for the bounty hunter to speak.

Ladan studied the windowless building, then closed his eyes. He did not hear her calling him. "Talia's not here," he calmly stated.

"How do you know?" Jeiel asked.

"Because I cannot feel her presence. Let's go on to the next house."

Zadok look at Jeiel, then shrugged. When he started walking, Ladan and Jeiel followed.

"Since when have you become telepathic?" Jeiel muttered, but Ladan heard the sarcasm in his voice.

"Since I met Talia."

Talia opened her eyes and scanned the Spartan room. A bed, a table, a chair. The walls were bare, the high window adorned with bars. She was a prisoner.

She was in hell.

Shifting restlessly on the bed, Talia tried to shut out the evil filling the air, shouting the misdeeds done in this place. The telepathic ability that had been a strength in the past now proved to be a liability.

Ladan! her heart shouted.

He was not here. Not within these walls or she would feel it.

Had he survived the attack? Or was his broken body still lying in that alley with no one to care or notice his death?

No, he was not dead. Her soul was still whole. If he had died she would feel the emptiness of his passing.

"Oh, so you're awake," a deep feminine voice commented.

Talia looked at the stout woman by the door. She was

plain, with pale eyes and washed-out brown hair. The woman's brow arched as she looked at the girl on the bed. "Selmet was right. You'll bring a high price." Not an ounce of understanding or compassion showed on the female's face.

She moved to Talia's side. "Ebes always manages to damage the goods," she grumbled, surveying Talia's face. "Sometimes, I wonder what that male uses for brains." Clasping Talia's chin, she titled it to the right. "It's a bad bruise. I don't know if I can disguise it with make-up."

She yanked Talia into a sitting position. On the nearby table sat a tray filled with small pots. Immediately, the woman dipped her fingers into one and applied the cream-colored mixture to Talia's chin.

"Close your eyes," she commanded.

"What are you doing?" Talia asked as the woman applied a lavender color to her eyelids.

"Making the most of what you have."

"I do not wish that."

The woman paused, took Talia's jaw in her hard, callused fingers, and forced it up. "You have no choice. If you're smart you'll realize that truth and reconcile yourself to it. You'll be happier once you do. Now close your eyes, girl, and let me finish my work."

Talia obeyed, but her mind rejected the admonishing words.

"What a mess your hair is," the woman complained, undoing Talia's braid. Talia remained passive until the woman tried to remove her circlet.

"No," Talia cried, breaking free from the female's grasp.

"I only wished to removed the circlet so I can dress your hair."

"Please allow me to keep it on—one last remnant of my former life." Talia hoped her reason would satisfy the woman. She was glad, also, that Ladan's band had not yet been discovered.

With a heavy sigh, the woman nodded.

Talia smiled in welcome relief. Her secret was still safe. But were her life and sanity?

Half an hour later, Talia was ushered out of the small room, down a long narrow hall to a large, well-lighted chamber. A raised platform stood in the center of the room, surrounded by rows of chairs. A man and a woman were on the stage. The short, balding man was encouraging the males sitting in the audience to raise their bids.

"Come, come, my friends, this female is worth more than 175 gold coins. Look, she has all her teeth, has no marks upon her, and will be a good breeder."

Talia closed her eyes, trying to shut out the ugly sight. She could feel the other woman's despair and shame, and knew the moment the woman was left alone she intended to end her life. Talia's mind reeled at the knowledge, and she rested her forehead on the wall, sick with sorrow.

"180," called a man in the back.

"Sold."

The auctioneer motioned for Talia. Ebes appeared at her side, seized her elbow and led her onto the stage. The low buzz of voices died, and Talia felt all eyes on her as she mounted the steps.

The carnality and vulgarity of the thoughts of the assembled men pounded Talia like a giant wave, nearly crushing her. She missed a step, and would have fallen if Ebes had not caught her elbow.

"This is our final piece of merchandise. And as you can see, I've saved the best for last. Perfect in every detail, this lovely female will fill some man's nights with countless delights. Now, I will take an opening bid of 100 gold coins."

"I wish to see her legs," one bidder called.

Selmet grabbed the material near Talia's knees and lifted the dress so all could see her shapely legs. The shock of his action nearly caused her to faint.

Calm yourself, Talia. Do not disgrace your heritage. You are Geala and will deal with this situation with grace and dignity.

Drawing in a deep breath, she pulled her shoulders back and looked straight ahead, trying to block out the bidding war raging around her. At the back of the room she saw the other men who had brought her to this place. When one of them nodded at her, Talia turned her head away.

"400."

She fought the lewd thoughts of the bidders, battering her senses.

. . . Her legs are shapely . . .

. . . Her breasts are just the right size to . . .

. . . I would like to . . .

Fight it, Talia. Fight it. Do not yield to their foulness. Think of the cool valley of home.

"550."

"Her fair skin and hair are a treasure, my friends."

"I'll pay 800 to taste her hidden delights."

Like an overloaded circuit, her mind snapped.

Ladan!

The cry of despair echoed through her being.

* * *

A half a block from the auction house Ladan heard Talia's cry. "She's at Selmet's," he called to Zadok. "We need to hurry." Ladan started to run down the street. "Where is the auction house?" he called over his shoulder.

"A block ahead," Zadok replied. "The black building with the yellow door on the corner."

Zadok and Jeiel raced to keep up with Ladan as he charged down the street and raced into the building. The three men burst past the startled guard into the main auction room.

"Sold for 1,000 gold coins to the Zicri ambassador. After paying, you may go to the back room and claim your property."

"You're wrong, Selmet. Nobody will claim the female but me." Ladan's words exploded in the room.

LADAN.

His eyes met hers, and he felt joy surge through her.

Everyone in the room turned toward the door where the tall male dressed in black leather stood. The violence vibrating from him snaked through the room, touching each man. The look of the two men behind him was no less threatening.

"Oh, and why is that?" Selmet asked, eyeing his guards at the rear of the room.

"Because the female's mine."

"I've only your word for that."

Ladan stepped forward. Jeiel and Zadok followed, their weapons ready for a fight. "Do you see my armband?"

"What about it?"

"The female bears a matching band. Show them, Talia."

Talia pushed up her right sleeve past her elbow, revealing the black and gold band. Ladan turned to the Zicri. "I'm Ladan. If you have not heard of me, Selmet—or any number of men in this room—can tell you I have the reputation as the most vicious bounty hunter in the star system. I've claimed the female as my mate. She possesses my armband. If you wish to dispute my ownership, I'll gladly accept the challenge. If not, renounce your rights to her before these witnesses."

The ambassador turned burning eyes on Selmet. "You will pay for my disgrace, Selmet." He addressed the gathered group. "I renounce any claim to this female," he ground out, then stormed from the room.

"Come, Talia," Ladan softly commanded, holding out his hand.

Ebes blocked her path. "I think not, bounty hunter. The female will stay here."

A feral smile curled Ladan's lips. "No one takes what is mine." The coldly spoken words froze all movement in the room.

Ladan carefully watched his opponent, waiting for the telltale sign of his attack. Ebes's hand started for his laser, but before he could lay his hand on it, Ladan grabbed his knife and threw it. The blade buried itself deep in Ebes's chest.

"Talia, get down," Ladan shouted as the room erupted in violence, and he dove for the floor.

The three guards in the back of the room rushed forward and were joined by four others, each armed with lasers. The bidders in the audience scattered, dodging the fire between the guards and Ladan and his men.

Ladan inched forward on his belly, using the discarded chairs for cover as he made his way toward Talia.

From behind a chair, a guard appeared and kicked the laser from Ladan's hand. Ladan scrambled to his knees and tackled the guard around the legs. They rolled together until Ladan was on top, his hands wrapped around the guard's neck. With one powerful jerk to the side, Ladan broke the man's neck, then grabbed the discarded laser.

"Behind you," Zadok yelled the warning at Ladan.

Ladan whirled and fired. Selmet crumpled at his feet, his gun still clutched in his hand. Ladan picked up the weapon and tucked it in his vest. Scanning the room, he saw only two guards crouched between chairs, the others lay on the floor motionless. When he glanced back at the stage, Talia was not there.

"Talia," he harshly whispered, running to the stage.

"Here, Ladan." She stood from her hiding place by the stairs.

Ladan's arm clamped around her waist and he squeezed her tightly. He only allowed himself a second to relish the feel of her before he released her.

The room was silent. Zadok and Jeiel rose from the positions behind overturned chairs.

"Are they all dead?" Ladan asked.

"Dead or disabled," Jeiel replied.

Ladan nodded to the two men. "My thanks."

Talia felt a prickling at the back of her neck. Danger. Without thinking she shoved Ladan out of the way just as Ebes threw the knife. She gasped as the fiery pain tore through her side. Looking down, she saw Ladan's black and gold knife buried deep in her flesh.

Here's a special offer for Zebra Historical Romance Readers!

GET 4 FREE HISTORICAL ROMANCE NOVELS

A $19.96 Value!

Passion, adventure and hours of pleasure delivered right to your doorstep!

HERE'S A SPECIAL INVITATION TO ENJOY TODAY'S FINEST HISTORICAL ROMANCES—ABSOLUTELY FREE! *(a $19.96 value)*

Now you can enjoy the latest Zebra Lovegram Historical Romances without even leaving your home with our convenient Zebra Home Subscription Service. Zebra Home Subscription Service offers you the following benefits that you don't want to miss:

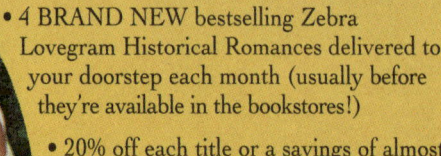

- 4 BRAND NEW bestselling Zebra Lovegram Historical Romances delivered to your doorstep each month (usually before they're available in the bookstores!)
- 20% off each title or a savings of almost $4.00 each month
- FREE home delivery
- A FREE monthly newsletter, *Zebra/Pinnacle Romance News* that features author profiles, contests, special member benefits, book previews and more
- No risks or obligations...in other words you can cancel whenever you wish with no questions asked

So join hundreds of thousands of readers who already belong to Zebra Home Subscription Service and enjoy the very best Historical Romances That Burn With The Fire of History!

And remember....there is no minimum purchase required. After you've enjoyed your initial FREE package of 4 books, you'll begin to receive monthly shipments of new Zebra titles. Each shipment will be yours to examine for 10 days and then if you decide to keep the books, you'll pay the preferred subscriber's price of just $4.00 per title. That's $16 for all 4 books with FREE home delivery! And if you want us to stop sending books, just say the word....it's that simple.

It's a no-lose proposition, so send for your 4 FREE books today!

4 FREE BOOKS

These books worth almost $20, are yours without cost or obligation when you fill out and mail this certificate.
(If the certificate is missing below, write to: Zebra Home Subscription Service, Inc., 120 Brighton Road, P.O. Box 5214, Clifton, New Jersey 07015-5214)

Complete and mail this card to receive 4 Free books!

YES! Please send me 4 Zebra Lovegram Historical Romances without cost or obligation. I understand that each month thereafter I will be able to preview 4 new Zebra Lovegram Historical Romances FREE for 10 days. Then if I decide to keep them, I will pay the money-saving preferred publisher's price of just $4.00 each...a total of $16. That's almost $4 less than the regular publisher's price, and there is never any additional charge for shipping and handling. I may return any shipment within 10 days and owe nothing, and I may cancel this subscription at any time. The 4 FREE books will be mine to keep in any case.

Name _____

Address _____ Apt. _____

City _____ State _____ Zip _____

Telephone ( ) _____

Signature _____

(If under 18, parent or guardian must sign.)

LF0597

Terms, offer and prices subject to change without notice. Subscription subject to acceptance by Zebra Home Subscription Service, Inc.. Zebra Home Subscription Service, Inc. reserves the right to reject any order or cancel any subscription.

A $19.96 value... absolutely FREE with no obligation to buy anything, ever!

ZEBRA HOME SUBSCRIPTION SERVICE, INC.

120 BRIGHTON ROAD

P.O. BOX 5214

CLIFTON, NEW JERSEY 07015-5214

AFFIX STAMP HERE

Ladan caught her as she collapsed. With her in his arms, he fired his laser, hitting Ebes directly in the heart. Holstering his weapon, he lightly stroked Talia's cheek.

"Why? Why did you do it?" he brokenly asked.

"Because he would have harmed you."

Burying his head between her shoulder and head, he breathed, "Oh, love."

"Ladan, let me fetch a doctor for her."

He raised his head to look at Zadok. "Hurry. Bring him to the vessel launch. I want to get off this cursed planet before anything else can go wrong."

Chapter 10

They had wounded her. Harmed what was his. Spilled the blood of his mate. If the scum were not already dead, Ladan would have ripped him limb from limb.

As he gazed down into Talia's pale face, another emotion sliced through his anger. Fear. A soul-chilling fear that he had never known before.

He carefully pulled the dagger—his dagger—from her side, his hand shaking. Blood flowed freely from the wound, coating his hands. The position of the injury, just below the ribs, would be a minor wound for him, but with Talia and her unknown heritage, he didn't know how her body would react.

Swiftly he loosened her belt, slid it up to cover the injury, then retied it. Her moan of pain ripped through him.

Tenderly, he scooped her up and carried her from the room. The blazing light in Ladan's eyes sent people scurrying out of his path. He blindly followed Jeiel out of the building and through the streets.

He wished he'd been the one wounded. The physical pain would have been easier to bear than seeing Talia suffer. Fortunately for his sanity, Zadok and the doctor were waiting at the ship when they arrived.

Ladan watched the doctor like a hawk as he tended Talia's wound. He never spoke a threat against the man, but the doctor kept glancing uneasily over his shoulder at Ladan. Finally, Zadok took pity on the quaking doctor and pulled Ladan across the room.

"Give the man some room to work, Ladan."

Ladan scowled. "What if she dies?"

"The wound doesn't look that serious."

"She took the blade meant for me."

"Yes. Not many females would be brave enough to do such a thing," Zadok added.

"Sirs," the doctor interrupted. "The woman will live." He handed Ladan a vial containing a half-dozen small green pills. "Give her one of these if she's in pain." The doctor closed his bag and started toward the door.

"Where do you think you're going?" Ladan snapped, his hand clamping down on the doctor's shoulder.

"W-why, home."

"No, my friend. You are coming to Ezion Geber with us. Since you and I don't know how Talia will react to the wound, if she will have a fever or some unknown complications, you will stay with us. After we are safely there, I'll have Jeiel bring you back to Alter."

"You can't. I'm wanted—"

Ladan smiled coldly. "Don't worry, friend. You won't have to leave the ship once we land. No one will turn you in."

The doctor started to protest, then caught sight of the uncompromising look in Ladan's eyes. "I'll stay."

"How wise of you," Ladan silkily replied, but the sound made the doctor shiver. He offered Zadok his hand. "Thanks for your help. I will relate your actions to Joakim."

Ladan turned back to Talia, everything and everyone else forgotten.

Ladan tenderly stroked the palm of Talia's left hand. The warmth of the blue star comforted him. The hum of the engines of Jeiel's ship was the only noise in the compartment. They'd been in route to Ezion Geber for the last star day.

The doctor hurried in and checked Talia's pupils and temperature. "I don't know what's normal for her, but to be on the safe side, I'll give her an injection to bring down her temperature."

Ladan stood with his arms folded over his chest and watched. The doctor's hands shook as he administered the dosage.

"Call me if anything changes," he said as he backed out the door.

Ladan's stance eased. Reaching down, he gently stroked Talia's cheek with the back of his naked fingers. She felt too warm. Quickly, he rinsed out a small cloth and bathed her face.

"Ladan, how is she?" Jeiel asked, entering the room.

"She's beginning to show signs of fever." Ladan's fingers ran into the circlet. Without hesitation, he removed the thin gold band.

Both men stared in stunned disbelief at the small

flower tattoo revealed on her forehead. Ladan immediately recognized it and its meaning.

"Ah, hell," Ladan savagely whispered. When Jeiel failed to say anything, he asked, "Do you recognize the symbol?"

"Yes. It's the rose poppy. Symbol of the royal family of Alcor."

"This one female is a mixture of my father's two most hated enemies. If he ever knew . . ."

"Ladan, what are you talking about?"

He held out his hands and Jeiel noticed, for the first time, that Ladan was without his gloves. Although the scaling was faint, he could see the rough skin. Jeiel's head jerked up.

"Dyne?"

"Yes," Ladan replied. "My father is Menoth."

Jeiel's jaw fell open, and he dropped into a chair. "It can't be."

"Wait, there's more." Ladan turned over his left hand.

Eyes wide, Jeiel stared at the blue star in Ladan's palm. After a long pause, he muttered, "You're just full of surprises, aren't you? Do you have any other bits of information you'd like to tell me?"

A rueful smile crossed Ladan's face. "Yeah, remember when I told you I was telepathic?"

Jeiel eyed him warily. "Yes."

"I meant it."

"Well, hell." Jeiel rubbed his forehead. "What's happening, Ladan? What's going on?"

Ladan sighed. "I wish I knew. Since I've known Talia, I appeared to have talents I never knew I possessed. Somehow, Talia has been able to touch that part of me that is Geala."

It was unbelievable—Ladan half Geala. Why, that was like the moon of Ezion Geber turning purple! "It's rather hard to take in what you've said."

"That's why I've kept it secret."

"Why do you fight against Menoth?"

"Because he killed my mother." From the biting tone of Ladan's words nothing else needed to be said. He looked down at Talia. "If Menoth ever discovers Talia's parentage, she will be dead."

Talia tried to ignore the burning pain in her side as she struggled up from the blackness of sleep.

"Ladan," she whispered.

"I'm here, little Geala."

His warm hand cupped her cheek, making her sigh in relief. She was safe. Ladan had found her.

Opening her eyes, she encountered his worried expression. "Do my features so displease you that you must frown?"

The fact she could tease him at this point rocked him. Talia was a fighter. "How do you feel?"

"Rather like the side of a mountain fell on me."

"I have something that will relieve the pain."

"No."

He leaned down and tenderly kissed her. Her warm lips welcomed him, and he was again enraged that anyone would dare try to take her from him.

When he pulled back, Talia glanced around the small compartment that obviously was part of a space vessel. Her eyes stopped on the narrow table by the bed. Her golden circlet lay beside a basin of water. Her eyes flew to his.

"Tell me your secret, Talia," he softly coaxed.

HUNTER'S HEART

Ladan had asked the question she dreaded. She could not lie, yet could not tell the truth.

"I'm your mate, now, Talia. Your secrets will be mine, and I'll guard them with my life."

She didn't doubt him. He would keep his promise and would die defending her.

When she still hesitated, he asked, "Talia, was your mother's name Teai?"

She gasped. "How did you know that? Did you read my mind?"

"No, I didn't read your mind. I recognized the tattoo on your forehead."

"My tattoo?"

"Yes, it's the royal design for the house of Usan, the rulers of Alcor."

Talia's eyes drifted closed. "I did not know."

"Somehow, that doesn't surprise me. Do you remember me telling you about Marshall Usan and his daughter Kami who negotiated the Ditans out of the Dyne Union into the Alliance?"

"Yes, I remember."

"Well, the people of Alcor are renowned warriors and their royal family was the guiding force in keeping the Alliance together to defeat the Dyne. Marshall was the last royal ruler. He had four daughters, each famous for her fighting ability. Kami was the eldest. Lyli and Syan were killed in battle, leaving only the youngest, Teai. Since you didn't react when I mentioned Kami, the only other alternative was that Teai was your mother."

"But how did she end up on Petar with my father?" Ladan's story was almost too farfetched to believe. Her mother a warrior?

"That's a good question. All I know is after the Alliance won, Menoth vowed to wipe out the house of Usan.

He offered a reward of 100,000 credits to anyone who would kill any member of the royal house. Marshall and Kami were murdered, but Teai disappeared and no one ever learned what happened to her."

Ladan shook his head. "Your parents must have made quite a pair. Like matter and anti-matter, I don't know how they mixed. What do you remember of your mother?"

"I was a small child when she died. All I can recall is that she was tall with blue eyes and long brown hair. And I remember her warning."

"What warning?"

"She told me to never allow the tattoo to be seen, that it identified me as her daughter, and her enemies would not hesitate to kill me, even if I was a child. She then followed the warning with laser gun training. Father did not approve."

Finally, her mother's words made sense. Now, in addition to her father's enemies, her mother had enemies who wished her dead. And the one person who most wanted her dead was her husband's father.

"It explains a lot, Talia, knowing who your mother was."

"What do you mean?"

"Aboard my ship when we fought the Dyne, your instincts guided you, just as they did when we were on Alter and Captain Neils captured us. Your fighting ability is natural." He smoothed his hand over her cheek. "Your mother was a great warrior."

His poor little tasha. Her parents were so opposite that he wondered how she ever found any peace within. His appearance in her life had not added to her ease, but only further stirred the boiling cauldron of her emotions.

With guilt weighing heavily upon his heart, he gently commanded, "Lay back and rest. I'll bring you something to eat after your nap."

Unable to sleep, Talia slipped from the bed and walked to the small oval window. Her mother had been a royal princess—and a warrior.

Talia wrapped her arms around her waist. She remembered her mother as a passionate person who loved to laugh and sing. Teai had daily practiced with her laser gun and spent several hours going through the movements of Kee, a method of fighting with hands and feet. Although her father never verbally rebuked her mother for her actions, it was obvious from his expressions that he didn't approve of his wife's behavior.

Finding out her mother's identity only added to Talia's inner turmoil. How could she resolve the peaceful teachings of her father with the warrior instincts of her mother?

The sound of the door sliding open broke into her thoughts. She turned and saw Jeiel carry in a tray of food. He set it on the table. Talia felt uncomfortable dressed only in a man's loose, flowing shirt and a blanket.

"We have not been properly introduced," the handsome man said. "I'm Jeiel."

"Ladan's friend. I am pleased to meet you, Jeiel." She glanced down at her attire, then at Jeiel. "I thank you for the use of your shirt."

He shrugged. "Think nothing of it. I must say, it looks much better on you than it ever did on me."

Talia blushed and looked away.

"If you're wondering where Ladan is, he is at the

controls, communicating with Ezion Geber. Our brave doctor is asleep in the co-pilot's chair.''

Talia smiled. She knew of the doctor's reluctance to be in the same compartment with Ladan.

She did not move toward the table but quietly observed Jeiel. Tall and slender, the man before her was devastatingly handsome. Whereas Ladan was dark, Jeiel was golden, from the top of his tawny head to the soles of his brown boots. Dressed in a flowing white shirt and snug tan pants, Jeiel outwardly did not fit her image of a bounty hunter. The laser strapped to his hip and the hilt of a knife tucked into his waistband were reminders, but it was the coldness of his blue eyes that reminded her of his profession. And although she knew he was a bounty hunter, Talia sensed the hardness in Jeiel stemmed from a different source than Ladan's. Perhaps the shadows of his past were not as dark as Ladan's.

"You're staring. Is there something you wish to know, Talia?"

Her eyes widened in surprise. "Forgive my breach of manners."

"Why were you staring?" He was tenacious, like Ladan.

"I have never seen a male with braids."

Jeiel ran his hands over the narrow braids that began at his temples and ended well past his shoulders. The rest of his blond hair hung loose. "The men of my world wear their hair in this fashion."

"And do they have the same facial hair as you?"

"Don't you like my mustache and beard?"

"Stop teasing Talia, Jeiel. She's never seen a male with a beard, let alone someone from Usol." Ladan's eyes went to Talia's. "What are you doing out of bed?" he gruffly demanded.

"I could not lie in bed one more instant, so I decided to gaze at the stars." She pointed out the window. "Is not that view of the heavens beautiful and peaceful? When I was a little girl, my father and I would sit out at night and gaze up into the sky. He would point out the different star groups, galaxies, and nebulae, naming them, telling me what he knew of each group. Do you see that spiral galaxy over there?"

Ladan and Jeiel followed her pointing finger.

"That is the Milky Way Galaxy. Our closest neighbor. I would stare up at that bright spot and wonder about the stars within, the planets that orbited the stars, and what kind of life they supported." She closed her eyes and rested her forehead on the window. "That was a thousand years ago," she whispered. "I am glad something has not changed."

Ladan slipped his arms around Talia's waist and drew her back against him.

"Nothing is constant, Talia. Everything changes unless it's dead. Those stars you see now might not even exist at this moment. What you see there is the past, not the future."

"I know," she sadly answered.

Each day Talia spent more time out of bed, moving about the ship. The strain of Alter's jungle had weakened her, and her recovery from her wound was slow. During that time, Talia and Jeiel talked. Although not forthcoming about his own personal history—a trait Talia assigned to all bounty hunters—Jeiel was a fount of information to Talia's thirsty soul. He told her how he and Ladan had met, the history of the Alliance and even shared what he knew about the royal family of Alcor. Even though Ladan rarely left her side, he allowed Jeiel to carry the brunt of the conversation, sitting back thoughtfully watching her.

Talia liked Jeiel. She was comfortable with him and enjoyed his quiet manner. Although he looked like a fierce warrior of some long-forgotten race, Talia sensed that his harshness resulted from some tragedy in his life, instead of existing as an inherent trait. And although she wanted to question him about it, she refused to probe into his past. Such was not the Geala way.

"When will we reach Ezion Geber?" she asked as she walked to the main control panel.

"In less than six star hours," Jeiel answered, glancing over his shoulder. He gestured toward the co-pilot's chair.

Talia held the blanket securely at her waist, guarding against its coming loose as she walked.

"Where's Ladan? Usually, he does not allow you out of his sight." As Jeiel looked around the cabin, he frowned. "For that matter, where's the doctor?"

"The doctor is in the corridor, asleep." When she saw his puzzled expression, she added, "He is holding a bottle of what Ladan called Mythinan brandy."

A chuckle rumbled in his chest. "It'll do it every time."

"Ladan is sleeping."

"It's about time," Jeiel said, checking the ship's coordinates. "I doubt he slept more than eight star hours over the last few days."

Eight star days—216 star hours. That's how long they had been in flight.

"You should be resting," Jeiel admonished.

"I cannot. I worry that I will be unable to reactivate the computer's defense shields."

"What?" Jeiel straightened in his chair, gaping at Talia.

His comical reaction almost made her laugh. It was the most emotion she'd seen the sanguine bounty hunter display since she had met him.

"You mean you don't know how to bring up the computer?" He sounded like he was strangling on a piece of meat.

"My father assured me that when I saw it I would know how to activate it."

"Terrific," he growled, then continued in a murmured voice. "We're all hanging our butts out to dry and don't even know if she can accomplish the task."

Talia was about to speak, when she sensed Ladan in the room.

"Don't worry, Jeiel," Ladan said, walking to Talia's side, "your backside will be safe. Talia will accomplish the task." No doubt or hesitation marred Ladan's voice, and Jeiel glared sourly at Ladan. Ignoring his friend's reaction, Ladan grasped Talia's hand and pulled her to her feet. "Come, you should be resting."

Jeiel grumbled something about Ladan's parentage as they left, but Ladan paid no attention. He guided Talia past the snoring doctor into the next compartment. After he put her in bed, he removed his leather pants and slid under the sheet with her. His nudity might shock her, but that was just too bad. He needed to feel her skin next to his, and, perhaps, she needed the reassurance his body provided. While she had been so desperately sick, his baser urges had slipped into the background, overridden by his concern.

As Talia recovered, so had his desires. It was torture

to watch her lips move as she ate, or observe the gentle sway of her hips as she walked, wrapped in a blanket, around the ship, or to see her shapely legs as she climbed in and out of bed.

Even though his lust burned a hole in his gut, Ladan felt uncertain about taking Talia again. She was a daughter of the royal house of Alcor and when that piece of information became known, what would happen? Would she be accorded the honor and duties of her position as a princess? What right did he, a savage bounty hunter, have to claim Talia as his mate? The match was ridiculous.

He reached out and gathered her into his arms. Her bare legs tangled with his, making him grit his teeth.

"Ladan?"

She laid her small, blue starred-hand on his chest, nearly causing him to jump out of bed from the shock of the contact.

"Yes," he croaked.

"I'm frightened. I know it is cowardly, and I have tried to fight it, but I cannot make the fear go away."

Tenderly, he kissed her forehead. "From the limited experience you've had with the outside world, I can understand your fear, but Ezion Geber is nothing like Alter 3 or that small mining town on Petar. The capital is a cool, beautiful city that was built by the Geala. You'll like it."

"But what if I cannot fulfill my father's request?"

His hands slid around her throat, his thumbs rubbing the small indenture at the base of her neck. "Perhaps you need something to take your mind off your worries," he breathed before capturing her lips in a burning kiss.

Her response didn't disappoint him. After a moment, she opened her mouth, welcoming his eager tongue. His doubts vanished as he gave into the consuming passion rising within. All he knew at this moment was that Talia was his.

Chapter 11

Talia gasped when she looked out the cockpit window and saw her father's home planet.

Like a brilliant jewel set on a bed of ebony, Gemmal appeared in the dark heavens. The deep blue of the oceans starkly contrasted with the three large land masses on the surface.

"Isn't it a sight to behold?" Jeiel commented.

"It is far lovelier than I imagined." She glanced up at Ladan, who stood behind the co-pilot's chair where she sat. "Where is Ezion Geber?"

Pointing, he said, "Do you see the continent shaped like a ragged disk that is entirely above the equator?"

She easily spotted it. "Yes."

"In the middle, about half-way up, is Ezion Geber. The weather is much the same as your valley on Petar, cool all year round."

It was Ladan's personal belief the Geala were pale because the light from their star was so weak in that northern clime. He definitely did not like the frigid days of Ezion Geber winters, favoring, instead, the warm climes reminiscent of his home planet. Alter 3's weather suited him just fine.

Talia fidgeted with the blanket covering her legs. Ladan understood Talia's plight and had already taken care of the situation. Leaning down, he whispered, "Why don't you go and dress your hair. When we arrive, there will be more appropriate clothing available."

Startled, her eyes flew to his.

"When I spoke to Ezion Geber earlier, I requested they have clothing waiting for you."

Talia's deep blue eyes shimmered with moisture. "Thank you."

After identifying his vessel and receiving permission to land, Jeiel guided his ship into one of the docking bays. Several officials were waiting on the platform as the hatch of the ship opened. Ladan greeted Joakim, then took the clothing from his assistant, Artis.

Ladan knocked once, then entered the compartment. He laid the clothing on the bed and stepped back.

Talia stared down in stunned disbelief at the pale yellow coat-dress, pants, and matching shoes. "How did you find these?" she asked in awe as she picked up one of the shoes and stroked the soft leather. Yellow. Her favorite color.

"Do they please you?"

"Yes," she replied breathlessly. Her face shone with pleasure. "I could not have asked for a more elegant outfit." His effort to obtain garb she would feel comfortable wearing had been no accident. He had carefully planned this surprise, she knew.

On impulse, she rose up on her toes and lightly kissed

him. "Thank you," she mumbled. After a short silence, she asked, "How did you obtain this style of clothing?"

A pleased grin split his face. "You forget, this is Gemmal, home planet of the Geala. And although the Geala are no longer here, their style of clothing is quite popular among those who dwell here. Now, hurry and dress. Joakim is eager to meet you."

A sickening knot formed in Talia's stomach. She prayed that she could do this thing requested of her. After changing, she glanced into the small mirror on the inside of one of the lockers lining the wall. The familiar clothing reassured her, easing her edginess.

She smoothed down a stray hair, tucking it back into the single braid. Her gold circlet was back in place. She and Ladan had decided that until Joakim could be informed of her true identity, she should continue to wear the gold band at all times.

Taking a deep breath to calm her shaking nerves, Talia pressed the door release. Immediately, she heard voices.

"The situation is critical. We've received word that the Dyne plan to launch an all-out attack sometime in the next six hours."

"I'm sorry it took so long, but there were many obstacles." Ladan refrained from mentioning his suspicions of a traitor at this time. He wanted to be alone with Joakim when he told him.

"Ladan."

The five men turned toward the soft sound. Talia's appearance robbed the men of speech. To Ladan, Talia looked every bit the princess she was, regal and elegant, cool and dignified. Talia smiled uneasily and moved to Ladan's side.

"This is the Geala?" asked the tall man with gray hair and beard.

"Show him your hand, Talia," Ladan softly ordered.

She held out her left hand, palm up. The older man shook his head.

"It's hard to believe she's Geala, but there's the evidence." His green eyes met Talia's. "I'm Joakim, the First Secretary of the Alliance. I'm pleased to meet you, young lady, and wish to extend my condolences on the death of your father. He was an old friend."

"Thank you, sir."

"Come, my dear, we need to hurry to the command center."

Ladan pulled Jeiel to one side. "See if you can find our brave doctor a ride back to Alter 3. I have a suspicion I'll need you here."

Talia looked around the docking bay. She counted seven vessels. Three looked to be commercial, the other four military. Ladan took her hand and escorted her to a large door. He pushed a button at the side, and it slid open to reveal a small chamber. The back half was made of a clear substance and a continuous bench ran around the walls.

Once all were inside, Joakim punched in coordinates on the wall panel by the door.

Trembling inside, Talia desperately wanted to touch Ladan in some way, but her Geala upbringing rose to the surface and she could not bring herself to do so in public.

Ladan felt Talia's dilemma. He wanted to wrap his arm around her shoulders and draw her close, but he knew it would be improper by her standards. Instead, he gave her a reassuring smile. *I'm with you, little Geala.*

She heard his thoughts clearly. Her eyes fluttered closed in relief. *Thank you.*

"What do think of our fair city, Talia?" Joakim asked, bringing her out of her musings.

She gazed out the back of the moving room at the city of Ezion Geber. Broad streets were lined with varying heights of buildings, composed entirely of cream-colored stone that gave a quiet harmony to the city. Covered bridges crossed the streets from one structure to another. The traffic on the street was light, and the clear tubes they were now in networked the city.

"What are we traveling in?" Talia asked, curious about this unique form of transportation.

"This is called TC—Tubal Conveyance. These high-density, clear plastic tunnels go throughout the city. The plastic will withstand a temperature of -150 degrees.

"Most of the city's traffic passes through the TC. The parts of the city not serviced by the TC are reached by the air-bus. Of course, individuals may own their own air vehicle, but only the very wealthy can afford them."

The moving booth stopped, and its portal slid open. In front of them was a gigantic set of double doors labeled with the words "Command Center." To the right stood a guard station with two men manning the post.

Talia took a step forward, then hesitated. She felt Ladan behind her, tall and strong. He found her clenched hand buried in the folds of her jacket and covered it with his, briefly squeezing. Immediately, he released her, making sure his small gesture of comfort went unnoticed.

Her sagging confidence restored, Talia moved toward the double doors.

The guard saluted Joakim.

HUNTER'S HEART

"Open the doors, sergeant. Help has arrived."

The soldier walked into the guard booth and flipped a lever. The doors opened to reveal a large room, filled with military people monitoring different panels and screens. In the center of the room was a three-dimensional holographic image of the star system. A clear panel, on which was another reproduction of the star system, divided the room.

"This is our command center, where all military operations are conducted. Here we keep track of what is happening within the star system, where the Dyne have attacked, and the current status of all battle stations," Joakim explained, leading Talia into the room. "The clear panel in the center of the room shows the different points of the defensive shield. As you can see, all are dark—which means they are inactive. The holographic image, next to the clear panel, is constantly updated to show the current traffic through the star system, and particularly around Gemmal." At that moment the laser image changed to show Gemmal and its star.

Talia slowly scanned the room, looking for something familiar. She noted the many different races of beings who wore the blue uniform of the Alliance forces. Finally, behind the clear panel, she spotted a welcome sight. She moved to the unmanned console, took a deep breath, then placed her hand on a darkened square. The terminal came to life, the square lighting up.

All activity in the room ceased. Joakim's eyes flew to the dividing panel. The lights of the defense shield remained dark. "The shields are not up," he said.

"Wait," Talia softly replied.

"Tactim," the computer's monotone voice uttered.

Much to everyone's surprise, Talia began to sing.

"Above the stars twinkle,
So bright and fine and free.
And among the stars that twinkle,
You'll find a part of me."

The soldier seated in the chair closest to Talia watched in amazement as each word she sang lit another square on the panel before him. The instant she stopped, the entire board before him came on, monitoring the defense shields. The clear panel behind Talia sprang to life, and a cheer went up as all realized the shields were on.

A quiet joy flooded Talia. Father had been correct. She had known the secret.

"I don't understand," the young soldier said.

"How did you know what to do?" Joakim asked.

Talia grinned. "My father built a duplicate of this part of the control panel that ran our small computer. In order to bring it up, I had to place my hand on the key, which was programmed to scan my palm and look for the blue star. If I put my right hand on the key, the machine would stay off. Next, the computer would ask for a verbal confirmation. I would sing the song my father devised for the machine. You see, each note on the musical scale is changed by the computer into a numerical equivalent, and that combined code turns the computer on. The song this machine asked for is different from the one I used with my machine."

"Then how did you know it?" Joakim asked.

"Tactim is a lullaby taught to all Geala children." She shook her head as she realized how ingenious her father's people had been. "The keys they used to turn on the computer, the blue star and the lullaby, were probably known by every Geala."

"Everyone but you," Ladan muttered.

"Ah, but I did know them. My father taught me the knowledge, he just never identified it as such."

"Well, why the hell not?" Ladan shot back. "What harm could it have done?" His resentment against Talia's father roared to life. With just a simple word Toaeth could have allayed Talia's fears. This protectiveness was foreign to Ladan.

"Perhaps, we should adjourn to a more private area so you two can discuss this matter," Joakim diplomatically suggested.

Subdued, Talia followed Joakim out of the command center, through a central hall, to his office in the main governmental building. Once he closed the door, he turned back to Ladan. "Do you have something you wish to discuss with Talia?"

Ladan felt like the universe's biggest fool and was in no mood for explanations. "No." He sprawled in one of the chairs in front of Joakim's desk. Talia quietly settled in the other one.

Joakim looked at Talia, then back at the bounty hunter. He sat down in the large blue chair behind his desk. "Then perhaps we should discuss the matter you wished to talk to me about in private."

Ladan held back a cynical smile. Joakim was a politician of the first order and knew when to press his case and when to withdraw. Obviously, he chose to withdraw and use a diversionary tactic. Well, he'd go along. "Talia, remove the circlet."

The slight tremble of her fingers betrayed her feelings as she pulled off the gold band. Joakim's eyes widened when he saw the rose poppy tattoo on Talia's forehead.

"Her mother was Teai?"

"Yes."

Joakim closed his eyes and fell back into his chair. He shook his head. "I knew that when Toaeth fled from Ezion Geber he took someone with him. Little did I know that it was Teai. But now that I think about it, Teai and Toaeth always had a sort of unusual relationship."

"What do you mean?" Talia asked, scooting forward in her chair, hungry for any information about her parents.

"Well, Teai was not as fiery as her sisters, but when it came to Toaeth she wasn't rational. Everything the man did seemed to annoy her. She would rage at his calm actions and his attitude. Toaeth endured her scathing remarks with a stoic smile. I guess all the signs of love were there, I just never paid attention. I would have loved to have seen them together. Talia, what were they like together?"

"I do not remember. My mother died when I was five."

"I'm sorry, my dear. Well, discovering a princess of the royal house of Alcor certainly puts a new twist on things, doesn't it, Ladan."

"There's more," Ladan stonily commented.

"Oh?"

"Talia is married."

Joakim's head jerked toward Talia. "To whom?"

"To me." The sound was hard and terse, chilling the room. "It was a declared union. I want you to record the marriage. It occurred on the 12th of Veadar, 1432." Ladan saw the regret in Joakim's eyes that Talia had already taken a mate.

Joakim fidgeted with a pen on his desk. "Of course I will record the union. Despite the marriage, I'm sure Talia's presence will reassure the Ditans. They have been nervous about the situation with the Dyne."

Unsettled by the tension between the two men, Talia turned to Joakim. "Sir, I can be of little help to you. I knew nothing of this war, nor of the Geala and Dyne or the royal house of Alcor, until Ladan told me." She ran her fingers over the edge of her circlet. "My parents sought to protect me by saying nothing of the raging tides around me. With a price on both their heads, I cannot disagree with their action. Therefore, sir, I would be woefully inadequate in any capacity as a diplomat. It is a role I do not wish to take."

Joakim pinned Ladan with a dark look. Ladan shook with ire as he read in the older man's eyes the question of why the marriage had to take place on the journey. Did Joakim think that he had forcefully taken Talia? Or married her because she was a daughter of the house of Alcor?

"Talia is very tired, Joakim, and requires rest. If you need us for anything, we will be at my residence within the city." He stood. Talia replaced her circlet, then joined him.

Joakim rushed from behind his desk. "I must announce Talia's presence to the council. I would like her to be there when they meet. That's the least you can do."

"All right. When is the meeting?" Ladan asked.

"Tonight. News will travel swiftly about our success in raising the shields, and I will have to speak to the people of Gemmal about the situation, but that will only happen after the council meeting."

"What time?"

"20.00 hours."

With a curt nod, Ladan pulled Talia from the office toward the TC station. Within seconds, the booth arrived and Ladan guided Talia inside. After punching in the coordinates for his residence, he sat on the bench next to Talia.

Talia's mind filled with Ladan's anger. She knew Joakim's suspicions had irritated Ladan, but how could she have reassured the older man that Ladan had not acted improperly? And how could she explain Ladan had only thought to save her sanity after she had killed? By his silence, Ladan saved her from the deep embarrassment her weakness caused.

She wanted to reach out and touch him, thank him for his thoughtfulness, but the dark scowl on his face told her he would not welcome the gesture at this moment. Instead, she looked out over the city, noticing for the first time that all the buildings were connected.

"Ladan, why are all the buildings constructed with covered passageways?"

His little Geala was still asking questions. At least something in the universe remained normal. "When your ancestors planned this city, they took into account what long, cold winters they experienced this far north, and since they did not function well in extreme physical discomfort, they connected every building to the next with passageways, assuring that they would never have to go out in the cold weather. As it happens, you can traverse the entire city and never have to go out into the open."

The TC stopped and Ladan hurried out. "My house is just a short way down the corridor."

Talia glanced around in awe at the clear corridor that ran the entire length of the street, with small offshoots at the door to each residence. She was so busy observing the lovely homes, trying to see in the windows, she failed to notice Ladan had stopped and plowed into him. He turned and caught her with his hands.

"I am sorry," she softly said, trying to explain her bumbling. "I was not looking where I was going."

"Obviously."

He punched a code into the key pad by the front door and it opened. The elegance of Ladan's house told of his wealth. Bounty hunting must be a profitable profession. The house well reflected its owner—harsh and Spartan. A few pieces of dark furniture were scattered in the main room. The cooking room was empty of all personal touches and food. The only place in the entire house that held Ladan's mark was the bedroom. On a table in the corner of the room stood a sculpture fashioned in black and gold. Ladan's design.

Slowly Talia moved to the large bed in the center of the room. Spread out over it were three outfits just like the one she was wearing. Her hand skimmed over the fine material of the coat-dresses.

"I hope you like these colors," Ladan said.

The pale colors of blue, green, and rose looked out of place in the masculine room. "They are exquisite."

A charged moment of silence arced between them. Ladan couldn't understand his illogical reactions. A knot of some unidentified emotion burned in his gut. He was ready to explode and needed some time alone. "While you bathe, I will check with Jeiel and see if the doctor found a transport home."

He strode toward the door, but Talia's words halted his escape. "Ladan."

"What?" He refused to face her.

"Thank you." Her words touched him like a lover's caress.

"You don't need to thank me for the clothes. It is a husband's job to provide for his mate."

"Thank you for not revealing my shame to Joakim.

You took his suspicion on yourself when what you did for me on Alter 3 was noble."

He spun around. His eyes glowed like liquid gold. "Understand, Talia, what I do isn't done out of kindness or gentleness or any other soft emotion. I act out of logic and what will serve my interest. I said nothing to Joakim because it was none of his damn business, and I resent him interfering in my affairs. I completed the quest he contracted me to do. He has nothing to complain about. He's greedy and wants what is mine. He can't have you."

He whirled and stomped out of the house. The walls of the building shook with the force he used to slam the front door.

Shaken by his violent outburst, Talia collapsed onto the bed. Ladan's words were said in the heat of anger, she told herself. He had not meant them. Yet, if she were honest with herself, she would have to acknowledge he had spoken the truth. Every one of his actions had been motivated by his driving need to finish his quest.

And yet, there was more between them than cold logic. Ordering these lovely garments to ease her mind had nothing to do with cold reasoning.

"There is more between us than you think, Ladan," she whispered aloud to the empty room. "What it is, I do not know, but as surely as there are heavens above, there is more. I would stake my life on it."

Chapter 12

Ladan glared daggers at the man who tried to enter the TC with him.

"Excuse me," the man squeaked, hastily backing away. "I believe I'll just wait for the next car."

The door closed and Ladan savagely punched in the first coordinate of the docking bay. The panel screamed and blinked in protest of the harsh treatment. Ladan gained control of his rage and entered the last grid number.

He refused to sit, but braced his legs wide apart, his arms folded across his massive chest. His simmering anger erupted and he slammed his fist against the clear wall, leaving a large dent in the plastic.

They were going to take her away from him. Or at least they were going to try. If he didn't miss his guess, Joakim was counting on Talia's Alcoran blood to enable her to divorce him and marry someone of Joakim's choosing. A political marriage to help the Alliance. Too bad Joakim's plans would fail. Talia may have been half Alcoran, but when it came to a mate, she was Geala through and through.

And yet, he knew Talia had a place within the elite of the Alliance, perhaps even a duty. Did he have any right to deny her the opportunity to find out?

The car jerked to a halt, bringing him out of his dark thoughts. He walked briskly to Jeiel's ship and entered the open hatch.

"Jeiel," he called, but there was no reply. His search of the vessel confirmed it was empty. Ladan threw himself in the pilot's seat to await his friend's return.

Talia. What was he going to do with her? He had not thought beyond the end of his quest, so any consideration of their future had not entered his mind. Did he want to continue taking bounties? Where would Talia stay while he was away, for he certainly couldn't take her with him on a hunt. Would she stay here on Gemmal? That would be the most logical assumption, but he didn't like the idea of her mingling with the power-hungry men who were among the elite of the Alliance.

And then there was that little matter of discovering who had betrayed him to Menoth. It had to be someone close to Joakim, who had access to the Alliance's secrets.

Hell, was anything simple?

"Ladan."

He turned toward the sound of Jeiel's voice.

"What are you doing here? I was planning to meet you at your house. I heard Talia was able to bring up the shields."

"Indeed, she did," Ladan affirmed proudly. "I never doubted her ability to do so, although you did."

"Then, why are you looking as mean as a Ditan night cat?"

"Joakim wants to use Talia as a peace-offering."

"A peace offering? To whom?"

"To disgruntled members of the Alliance. A royal princess is suddenly dropped in the old geezer's lap. The only problem is she's already married. He'd like Talia to be free so he could marry her off to some leader to secure his power."

Jeiel's eyes narrowed as he studied his friend. "Did Joakim say this, or did you just interpret his actions as such?"

It was the wrong thing to say. Ladan gave him a dark look. "You forget, friend, my instincts are what made me the best bounty hunter in this star system."

Jeiel sat down in the co-pilot's chair. "What led you to believe Joakim disapproves of your marriage to Talia?"

"His eyes told me. At this point, he doesn't know which of Talia's sides is stronger, the Alcoran or the Geala. He hopes it's the Alcoran. That way, he can separate her from me. That won't happen. There's a council meeting tonight where he is going to introduce Talia. I'd like you to be there."

"I'd be honored."

"I have another problem, Jeiel. There's a traitor among the top members of the Alliance. The Dyne knew too much of my movements. I want to find out who it is."

Ladan's tone indicated the culprit would face a harsh death the moment Ladan learned his identity.

"Have you discussed this with Joakim?"

"No."

"Why? Do you suspect him?" Jeiel asked.

"Joakim's no traitor. A pompous politician, but not a traitor."

"Then why didn't you tell him?"

"Because I wasn't in the mood. Besides, I wanted some time to look into the matter myself before going to him."

"What do you want me to do?" Jeiel asked.

"Go to some of the bars the military frequent. Mingle. See if there's been any strange transmissions from the planet's surface in the past thirty star days."

"All right, Ladan. I'll see what I can find out."

Ladan glanced around the vessel. "What did you do with the good doctor?"

Jeiel grinned. "Do you know Xeat?"

Ladan's lips quivered, then broke into a wide, smile. "The Black Pirate?"

"The same. He was in port and going to Alter. He took the doctor with him over the doctor's protest."

"Well, I promised him I'd get him back to Alter, I just never mentioned how."

Jeiel leaned back in the co-pilot's chair and stared at the opened hatch through which Ladan had just disappeared. His friend was acting in irrational manner. The cold anger in Ladan's voice when he talked about Joakim spoke of a coming storm. It was simply a matter of time before the tempest broke.

Ladan's peculiar actions and reactions told Jeiel that there was something new and different about Ladan's relationship with Talia. Something that had never existed before with any other woman. Certainly, Talia had touched a part of Ladan on one else had ever reached. It also proved Ladan had a heart, which disspelled the commonly held belief that Ladan had no heart and knew no emotion other than anger.

But what was this thing the existed between Talia and Ladan?

Love.

Now where had that stupid notion come from. Love was the female word for lust. There was no such thing as love.

Then what of the emotions that burn between Ladan and Talia? a voice in his head whispered.

"Lust," he muttered.

Lust? Who ever heard of a Geala who lusted?

Jeiel stood and shook off the silly thoughts. He needed to find a bar, mix among the officers, and see what they knew. He had no time for these useless thoughts of love.

Ladan left Jeiel behind at the docking bay, intending to go straight back to his house, but at the last minute decided to visit the trading center of the city. Since it was summer and the weather warm and inviting, some of the merchants set up counters outside their neat shops. Ladan walked past the street of clothiers, glassblowers, and food merchants to the row of artisans.

A small laser beam monitored the door of the shop, sounding a bell when the beam was interrupted as a customer entered. A middle-aged man emerged from the curtained back of the store.

"Ladan," he cheerfully greeted. "Are you here to pick up your medallion? The work you wanted done is finished."

Until the jeweler spoke the words, Ladan had no idea what had drawn him to this place. Now he knew he'd come to claim the medallion. Talia would wear his mark in plain view of all at the council meeting. There would be no mistaking the fact that she was taken.

"Yes. I'm here for the disc."

The jeweler disappeared behind the curtain. When he returned, he placed the medal in Ladan's gloved palm.

Carefully, Ladan examined the intricate working of black and gold on the surface of the disc. The craftsmanship was superb, but that was why he came to Rofe. He expected no less. His fingertips slid over the heavy links in the gold chain.

He frowned. The chain was too harsh for Talia.

"I will need a finer chain. Do you have one?"

Rofe scratched behind his ear. "I think. . ." He fumbled through several drawers behind the display counter. "Here it is." He held up an elegant but sturdy chain. The links were not oval but crimped at one end. "You are fortunate the disc is so light that this chain will easily carry its weight."

Once Ladan approved, the jeweler swiftly exchanged the chains. Ladan slipped the medallion in his vest pocket. As he left the shop, he decided to bring Talia here and allow her to select some pieces of jewelry that would please her.

All women liked expensive jewelry. *All*, his mind hissed, *except Geala females*. They considered sparkling gems crass.

Talia rubbed her aching side. Arms wrapped around her waist to ease her pain, she stood and walked around Ladan's bedroom. Besides the large bed, a table and chair were the only pieces of furniture in the room. The walls were stark white, the floor covering—a soft material she had never seen—gray. The austere room reflected Ladan's isolation from others, his complete alienation from the softer emotions of kindness, gentleness and love.

"My poor Ladan, have you known any love in your lifetime?" she whispered, her heart aching for him.

She moved to the two doors set in the wall, hoping to find the bathing room. The first turned out to be a closet. Black was the main color of the clothes, but there were three white shirts. She'd like to see Ladan in one of those shirts.

The second door was the bathing chamber. Here, too, the room contained only the basic necessities—a bar of soap, drying cloths, a comb, a straight edge, all of the highest quality—but nothing that was a reflection of the man.

She quickly bathed and washed her hair. Wrapped in one of the large, fluffy drying squares, Talia sat on the bed to work out the tangles in her waist-length hair. Her eyes teared as the comb caught a snag. Suddenly she sensed Ladan's presence and stopped struggling with the knot.

"Here, let me do that." He held out his hand for the comb.

Surely she had heard him incorrectly.

Ladan gently took the comb from her numb fingers and sat behind her on the bed. She felt him remove his gloves, then run his fingers through her long golden mane, working out the major knots. Chills danced down her spine and her skin felt tight as his fingers caressed her scalp.

"If you start at the bottom and work your way up, you will not have as many tangles." His deep voice only added to the web of magic surrounding her.

How does he know that? Talia dreamily thought.

"I know because I watched my mother dress her hair. When I asked her why she started at the bottom, she told me it was the easiest way to deal with the tangles."

As he worked the comb through her hair, Talia realized that Ladan had read her mind, but from his reaction he had not realized he'd received the telepathic communication. He probably thought she'd spoken.

Ladan.

"Yes, Talia."

You are reading my mind.

His hands stilled in her hair. This was not what he wanted nor planned, but the bond between them was growing stronger at light speed. Now, not only in times of distress or emergency could he hear her telepathically, but sitting casually on the bed he could receive her thoughts.

He stood and handed her the comb. "I'm going to bathe before we leave. Your hair will dry faster if you sit on the balcony off the main room."

Rising, she headed for the door.

"Talia."

"Yes, Ladan." Her body tensed as she faced him.

Reaching into his pocket, he withdrew the medallion. "I want you to wear this tonight."

Talia glanced down at the armband, which she had not removed since he had placed it there, then at Ladan. He shifted, but said nothing.

Her fingers brushed his palm as she took the disc. A bolt of electricity ran up her arm. "If you wish."

"I do." He disappeared into the bathing chamber.

Talia moved through the main room to the balcony in a daze. Day was fading, coloring the city with reds, golds, and long shadows. Lights appeared in the buildings, gleaming counterpoints to the darkening sky. A soft wind blew through her hair, bringing with it the tangy smell of the tall trees growing on the hill below.

Her hand tightened around the gold medallion. Ladan wanted all to see that she belonged to him, but why did he feel the need to show his possession? Did he doubt her, think her wavering in her commitment to him? She would wear the disc and wear it with pride.

The wind blew several strands across her face. As she pushed them away, she was reminded of Ladan's tender combing of her hair. He had shocked her with his actions. He proclaimed himself to be a heartless hunter, and yet he had sat upon the bed and gently worked the tangles from her hair. He had done other things for her. He had ordered the clothes here in Ezion Geber, allowed her to keep the catwig on Alter, had been sensitive to her feelings the morning after they had lain together. All those actions were motivated out of concern for her welfare.

The seeds of love and tenderness were still in Ladan. They had not been destroyed, simply never allowed to blossom. He was beginning to change, to soften. The Geala qualities he possessed were asserting themselves. His telepathic ability was almost as strong as hers. If they kept up this pace, neither of them would have to utter a word to communicate.

In spite of this softening, Talia sensed an inner struggle in Ladan, one he tried to shield from her. There was an area of his soul where no light ever penetrated. Even as they grew closer, that part of Ladan withdrew. And it was that dark area of his soul she feared.

* * *

Ladan paced around the couch in the main room, waiting for Talia. He ran his hand under the collar of his white shirt, then rolled his shoulders, trying to get the material to lie flat. He still wore his black leather vest and pants, but in deference to the state occasion, he left off the chest belts. Instead, he strapped a scabbard, worked with his design, to his right thigh. His shoulder-length hair was tied at his nape with a black thong.

He fingered the hilt of the knife. What was keeping her?

At the sound of the door opening, he whirled. His eyes widened in stunned surprise as Talia emerged from the bed chamber. He had commanded that she wear the medallion, but he thought she'd wear it around her neck. Instead the disc lay on her forehead, covering the tattoo, the chain disappearing into her elaborately braided hair.

"Ladan, is something amiss?" She glanced down at the pale blue outfit.

He cleared his throat. "No. It's just that I expected you to wear the medallion around your neck."

She touched the disc on her forehead. "Are you displeased?"

He shook his head. "Why did you wear it in your hair?"

"Father always disliked outward adornment."

He'd ordered her to wear something her race frowned upon. Her inventive solution of wearing it in place of her circlet won his admiration.

"You are lovely." Her shy smile sizzled through him like a drop of water on a hot rock, unleashing his passion. The memory of her sitting on the bed, her creamy white shoulders bare above the drying cloth, flashed through his brain, further tormenting him. What he wanted at this moment was to take her back into the other room, lay her on the bed and—

Talia gasped.

A dull red stained Ladan's cheeks. He grabbed her arm and led her to the front door. "That's what happens when you're telepathic. You intrude into personal thoughts that you have no business knowing."

The council chamber was full by the time they arrived, but the meeting had not started. Talia glanced around in awe of the luxurious surrounding. At the far end of the room, a raised platform supported a long table with nine chairs, one for each member of the Alliance. Below the head table were rows of seats for the audience to hear the council meeting. Talia studied each ambassador as he stood behind his chair on the platform.

"Be careful, your curiosity is showing," Ladan whispered in Talia's ear. The twinkle in his eye told Talia he was teasing instead of rebuking her, as her father would have.

"Sometimes I feel as if I have been reborn and am experiencing everything for the first time. I do not know what to do with all the questions I have."

"It seems to me you ask them."

Talia's lips twitched with mirth, and she swallowed a giggle. "Do not encourage my misbehavior," she lightly scolded.

Through the crowd, Talia spotted Joakim and watched him hurry toward them. Joakim's broad smile slipped for an instant when his eyes rested on the medallion adorning her forehead. He glanced at Ladan, whose only reaction was a slight dip of his head.

Talia felt the tug-of-war between the two personalities in spite of her curiosity about the new things around her. "Mr. First Secretary, I hope we are not late."

"Only a few minutes, my dear."

"The fault is mine," Talia answered. "I am not used to having to pace myself by a measured time."

Joakim's expression was sympathetic. "I know, but soon it will seem second nature to you."

I doubt it, she silently answered, only to have Ladan nudge her.

"Shame on you for such a thought," he murmured in her ear.

Talia felt the heat rise up her throat and spread to her cheeks. Joakim opened his mouth, but Talia cut him off. "Perhaps we should proceed with the meeting."

Joakim led Talia to the first row, then took the middle chair behind the main table. With a single clap of his hands, the milling crowd found seats, and the ambassadors took their places.

"I wish to announce that earlier this day, at 01.24, the Alliance's defense shields were raised, cutting off a planned attack from the Dyne. When the forces of the Dyne Union ran into the shields, most dispersed. Our fighters engaged those who remained, and we soundly defeated them. I then ordered the fighters to pursue the fleeing enemy. I am happy to report none of the Dyne ships escaped."

A gigantic roar went up from the crowd. In the midst of the applause and cheers, Talia felt a pair of hostile eyes upon her. She glanced around the room. Ladan's hand slipped under her elbow, and he lightly squeezed her arm.

Joakim raised his hand to restore order. When the room was calm again, he continued. "All of you know that our only chance to survive was to find the last living Geala. That was the quest I gave Ladan. He succeeded, but he brought back a far different individual than I expected."

Rising, he came around the table to Talia's side. After urging her to stand, he led her to the platform. "Ambassadors, my fellow citizens, I would like to introduce you to Talia, daughter of Toaeth and Teai of the House of Alcor."

A murmur ran through the room. The ambassador from Ditan, Dimas, stood. He was tall, with pale blue skin, white flowing hair, and bushy eyebrows. "I would like to see proof."

Ladan shot out of his chair to Talia's side. "She is making no claim for power. She has done her duty to the Alliance at the high personal price of her father's life. She owes you nothing else."

"Perhaps we can adjourn to the reception room and Dimas can talk to Talia herself," Joakim hastily said. After receiving approval from both Ladan and the ambassador, Joakim herded everyone into an adjoining chamber where a buffet was set up.

Ladan held Talia back as the guests filed out around them. When the room was empty, Dimas moved in front of Talia. When he reached out to touch the disc on Talia's forehead, Ladan stepped between them.

"She has nothing to prove to you."

"But Joakim said—"

"Joakim has no authority over my wife."

The man's eyes widened and he turned to Joakim. "Is this true?"

"Yes." Joakim heavily sighed and rubbed his neck.

The ambassador stepped back. "That's too bad, if what you say is true. She could have made an advantageous marriage."

Ladan's fingers curled around the hilt of his knife and a murdering rage filled his head.

No, Ladan.

Her cry stopped him. He took a deep breath and slowly relaxed. Dimas bowed and left.

Joakim sighed heavily. "Perhaps we should join the others."

Ladan rounded on Joakim. "I refuse to allow Talia to be bartered for the further security of the Alliance. She is mine. The Geala bonding between us is complete. You have always treated me fairly, Joakim, and that is all that has kept my temper in check these last few minutes, but don't press me any further."

The older man studied Ladan, his shrewd eyes missing nothing. "As you wish, Ladan. But you cannot blame an old man for being excited about discovering a princess of the House of Alcor. It could do much to strengthen the Alliance."

"Joakim." The deadly warning in Ladan's voice even shook Talia.

"All right, Ladan, you win. But you can't have any objection to the others meeting Talia."

"As long as they don't continue to demand proof of her claims."

"Of course," Joakim hastily reassured him.

"I hope you have something besides meat at your buffet," Ladan muttered, ushering Talia into the reception. "My wife has an aversion to eating flesh."

Chapter 13

Talia felt a frisson of warning race down her spine. She paused in her conversation with the Mizaran official and scanned the room, searching for the source of the hostile feelings.

Ladan immediately picked up on her disquiet. "Would you excuse us, Neqet?"

He pulled Talia away from the milling crowd into a quiet corner. "What's wrong?" he softly asked.

"I do not know, but someone in this room—I feel danger."

"Can you identify the source?"

She shook her head. "I just have a feeling that someone in this room wishes evil done."

Ladan searched the crowd, found Jeiel, and motioned to him. When Jeiel joined them, Ladan asked, "Did you discover anything?"

"No. The tavern was empty at this time of the day."

"I want you to stay with Talia while I mingle with the guests."

"It will be my pleasure to be with the loveliest female in the room." Jeiel laughed at Ladan's disgruntled expression. He leaned close to Talia. "I believe he's jealous."

"Of what could he be jealous?"

"You are a comely female, Talia. Any male would fight to keep you."

Her brows knitted in a frown.

"You are not used to being complimented on your comeliness, are you?"

"It is the heart that determines beauty."

"Perhaps that's why I'm so ugly."

"Oh, no," she softly cried, remorse piercing her soul. "I meant no such thing. Yours is a heart wounded, but not dark."

Jeiel froze, and Talia moaned at her blunder. Each time she spoke she made the situation worse. "I apologize for my rudeness."

His expression bleak, Jeiel said, "You are right." He held out his hand. "Would you like something to eat?"

Relieved that he had given her a way of escaping her embarrassment, she nodded and followed him to the buffet table. The colorful array of food pleased Talia's eyes. Blue, yellow, and purple fruits. White meat from the sea, dark meat from the local foul. Breads, twisted, and sweet, wrapped around some unknown food.

Talia took several pieces of the cut daffus fruit. "This is the only thing I recognize," she whispered to Jeiel.

"Would you like me to identify the other items?" Jeiel asked out of the corner of his mouth.

"Yes," Talia eagerly replied.

Again, the warning that something was wrong

slammed into Talia, and she turned, scanning the room. She saw Bartis, the Cetus ambassador, take the offered silver goblet from a tray that a servant held. Suddenly, she knew what was wrong and dashed across the room to knock the drink out of the ambassador's hand before he could taste it. She whirled and swept all the goblets off the tray.

Silence reigned, everyone in the room staring agog at Talia. Ladan lunged forward and grabbed the servant by the scruff of the neck. If he didn't miss his guess, the wine had been poisoned, and only Talia, with her telepathic ability, was able to pick up on it before every ambassador in the Alliance lay dead.

"Why did you poison the wine?" Ladan harshly demanded. When the hunched man failed to answer, Ladan shook him so hard that Talia was afraid the man's neck would snap.

"Ladan, allow the man to answer."

He heard Talia's soft command and released the servant. But before he could question the man further, she moved between them.

"Who handed the tray to you?" Talia gently asked.

"Some man. But I swear I've never seen him before in my life."

"And did you not find it odd that this unknown man gave you this tray?"

"No. I usually work in the kitchens, but someone was sick, and I was asked to serve."

"Is the man in this room?" Ladan demanded, impatient with the slow progress.

The servant jumped back, then carefully looked at each face in the room. "No."

"Were you given any specific instructions?" Ladan

wanted everyone in the room to know the extent of the treachery done this night.

"Yes. I was told this was a special wine, to be given only to the council members."

Murmurs and gasps ran through the crowd. Ladan bent down and picked up one of the goblets. A small amount of liquid remained in the bottom. After sniffing, he handed the cup to Joakim.

"The smell is faint, but if you have your lab test this, I think you will discover Tokia poison."

Several women screamed. One fainted. A mad buzz claimed the room. The Cetus representative looked at Talia. "How did she know it was poisoned?" The question brought quiet to the room.

Ladan stood behind Talia and placed his hands on her shoulders. "Because my wife is only half Geala, her telepathic ability is somewhat altered from a full-blooded Geala. Talia sensed the wrong that was to be wrought in this room tonight but had trouble identifying it. You are fortunate she was able to discern it before it was too late."

The Ditan ambassador moved to Talia's side, took her hand and kissed it. "You acted as a true daughter of your house. Your grandfather would have been proud of your swift reactions this night. If I may ever be of service to you, please contact me."

In rapid succession, each of the remaining eight ambassadors paid homage to Talia. Flustered and embarrassed by the uproar, Talia stiffly thanked each man for his support.

Knowing Talia was fast losing her composure, Ladan bid the gathering a good evening and led her from the room. He motioned for Jeiel to follow.

As they waited for the TC, Ladan felt tremors begin

to shake Talia's body. He cursed the slow car. When the door slid open, he pulled Talia inside and wrapped his arms around her, gently placing her head on his shoulder. Jeiel keyed in the coordinates of Ladan's house.

"Did you see anyone leave?" Ladan asked his friend, while his hand stroked Talia's back.

Jeiel heard Talia's muffled sob and tried to ignore it. "No."

"I didn't, either. Yet I have the feeling someone slipped from that room. If we can discover who it was, I think we'll have found our traitor."

"Are you going to tell Joakim now?"

"I think he already knows, but tomorrow I'll speak with him."

Jeiel didn't disembark with Ladan and Talia, but continued on to the docking bays. Ladan swept Talia into his arms and walked to his house. He did not let go of her once inside, but, instead, carried her to the bed. Tenderly, he undressed her and placed her under the covers. He stripped and joined her. His nimble fingers worked through her hair, combing out the elaborate braids.

He loved the silk of her hair, the softness of her skin, her light smell that was clean and fresh and all woman.

He pulled the medallion from her hair and kissed the tattoo on her forehead. He smoothed his thumbs over her cheeks, then he reached down and grasped her left palm with his.

The touching of blue star to blue star finally broke the chills that racked her body. She snuggled closer to Ladan's large frame.

"Can you tell me what happened?" he asked.

"They have accepted me. They think my actions

tonight were courageous. I fulfill their ideal of what a princess should be."

"And that bothers you? Most would enjoy the homage given you this night."

She raised her head and looked at him. "Why?"

"Power, Talia. Everyone in the universe wants power."

Sitting, she pulled the sheet over her raised knees, then wrapped her arms around her legs, resting her chin on her knees. "No, I do not believe that. The Geala did not want power."

"And they're all dead," Ladan flung back.

She placed her forehead on her knees, hiding her face in the sheet. Ladan placed his hand on her bare back.

"I'm sorry, Talia, but harshness is part of me."

She turned to him, her hair swinging wildly about her shoulders. "No."

A bark of laughter tore from Ladan's throat. "You're wrong, Talia."

"What I meant to say was that although you have been taught to be harsh, with me you have been gentle."

"Gentle? I've cursed you and your parents, been impatient and short with you."

"That is true." She could not stop her grin. "But you have also helped me, thought of my needs, kept me from madness. That is not cruelty."

Ladan flopped down, then pulled Talia into his embrace. "Now, tell me what was bothering you before we began this senseless discussion of power and cruelty."

Talia tried to recapture her earlier thoughts. "I do not understand why I behaved so poorly. To cry is intolerable." Her voice broke.

"Your Alcoran half is asserting itself, Talia. If you had not acted on your instinct, those ambassadors would be dead. Your reaction in the TC was simply your Geala mind trying to absorb what happened."

"I feel as if I am being torn in two."

He gently rubbed her back. "Give yourself some time to find the path through this turmoil."

He thought she'd gone to sleep when he heard her whisper, "The evil is still there, Ladan. We did not defeat it. Only delayed it."

"I know." *You're their main target.*

He did not speak the last. He did not have to. Talia heard him clearly.

Jeiel strode into the poorly lit bar, just a few streets away from the docking bays. Bars in this part of town were usually frequented by enlisted men and noncoms. And if he wanted to know if anything was amiss within the military, this was the place to discover it.

Jeiel ordered a Mizan beer and took a seat in the corner of the room to observed the activity in the room. He heard bits of different conversations, but nothing that would help in his quest.

After an hour of nursing his drink, an old ally entered the bar and, after ordering a drink, turned and spotted Jeiel.

"What brings you to this part of the star system?" David Seneth asked as he took a seat at the table with Jeiel.

"I'm helping an old friend." Jeiel wondered what David, a captain in the military, was doing at this particular bar.

"Ah, yes, I heard a rumor that you brought Ladan and the princess back to Gemmal."

The way David phrased his answer put Jeiel on alert. "I guess there nothing that's a secret on this planet."

David lifted the drink to his lips. "It appears not."

Jeiel sensed a buried anger in the man. "This is an unusual place for you to come."

A muscle jumped in David's cheek. "I could say the same for you. You don't like to mix in bars unless your looking for someone."

"Maybe," Jeiel said, fingering the empty glass in front of him, "you and I are here for the same reason."

The captain's brow lifted. "You're not going to get me to talk first like you did the last time, bounty hunter. I had a hell of a time explaining how my prisoner was snatched out of my detention ship and ended up being take to Theams."

The man had a point. Jeiel had used the information David gave him to steal the killer and take him back to his home planet for a large bounty. But David's protest lack rancor.

When David was a green lieutenant straight out of the military college Jeiel had saved David's butt by warning him of a planned attack on the base he was stationed. David had warned the forces, the local revolt was quashed, and David's career had taken off. Jeiel had never mentioned the incident, had never requested anything from David, but Jeiel always knew that at some point David would pay him back. Now was the time.

Jeiel's gaze met David's. "All right. You know that tonight someone tried to poison all the Alliance ambassadors at a reception."

A curse slipped from David's.

"I'm looking for anything unusual that has happened

within your ranks in the last lunar month." Jeiel leaned forward. "Do you know something?"

"I don't, but today someone contacted me about several strange occurrences. That's why I'm here. To meet with him."

"Mind if I stay and listen in?" Jeiel asked.

"Only if you promise not to kidnap my source."

"You have my word to behave."

David simply laughed.

Talia slipped quietly from the bed. She glanced down at her bare form and knew she could not speak to the Creator in this state of undress. Her eyes fell on Ladan's shirt. With trembling fingers, she picked it up and put it on. She silently moved into the main room to stand before the windows. The horizon blazed with color as morning overtook night.

She had never thought past the completion of her father's mission. Now, with it successfully finished, her future was unsure.

She was confused. A stranger inhabited her body. Things that seemed to come instinctively now—such as knocking away the poisoned drink—would have been foreign to her just days ago. The changes in her had come so swiftly and dramatically that she felt as unstable as dimers in Argon gas.

The fighting instinct that had prompted her actions last night was still unfamiliar and uncomfortable for her to deal with. The Alliance leadership's sudden reversal of attitude toward her, from openly doubtful to laying laurels at her feet, had been too much for her.

Her father had told her the Creator bestows favor

and honor. It came not from others. So what was she to think of the praise this night?

She was lost, all direction gone. She bowed her head. *Creator, help me.*

Ladan knew the instant Talia left the bed, but he allowed her time alone to sort through her troubled emotions. Admittedly, his emotions were as turbulent as hers. He wasn't surprised Menoth had tried to poison the leaders of the Alliance, just amazed he'd been able to get as far as he did. What bothered Ladan was the fuss afterward, with everyone falling all over themselves to ingratiate themselves into Talia's good graces. He had almost punched the Mizaran ambassador after he fervently kissed Talia's hand.

They all wanted a piece of this princess, and if he was honest with himself, he knew she belonged to them. Her fate should've been to marry a high-ranking, powerful male with a spotless reputation, instead of a mean, contemptible bounty hunter, the breed son of the enemy forces.

In spite of these logical arguments, Ladan's heart refused to release his claim on her. She was his.

He bounded out of bed and dressed in his discarded pants. When he entered the main room, his breath caught at the sight of Talia standing at the window, her shapely legs showing beneath the edge of his shirt, the bright light outlining her body through the white material, and her golden hair spilling down past her waist.

The doorbell chimed, breaking into Ladan's thoughts. At the door stood Jeiel, hot breakfast rolls and fresh fruit in his hands. Ladan scowled at him.

"And good morning to you, my friend," Jeiel said as

he entered. "Where's Talia? I've brought you something to eat." He stopped on the last of the four steps, leading from the front landing to the main room, his eyes wide as he looked at Talia.

She turned and smiled at Jeiel, until she noticed Ladan's thunderous look.

"You need some proper clothes," Ladan curtly announced, acutely aware of Talia's state of undress. "Dress, and I'll take you shopping."

Talia disappeared without a word, but Jeiel was not so obliging.

"You can be a real bastard when you want, Ladan. Your reputation is well-earned."

"You push our friendship, Jeiel."

"Yes, but I can't stand by and watch you take out your confusion on the innocent. And Talia's innocent."

Ladan cursed violently. "I need some ginter tea."

Jeiel cringed. "I wish none."

Ladan smiled in spite of his dark mood. "You're a woman, Jeiel. Even Talia likes ginter." At the mention of Talia, his mouth hardened.

Jeiel set the food down on the empty counter while Ladan pulled a pan from a cabinet.

"Have you heard anything?" Ladan rummaged through the cabinets, searching for the tea.

"Yes. I met an officer last night who told me that there have been several unauthorized transmissions from the planet's surface. The messages were coded, and they have not broken the code. But that is not the most interesting part. Several weeks ago, one of the control operators was tracking a cargo vessel entering Gemmal's atmosphere, when suddenly he passed out. When he woke up, the screen was empty and there was no sign of the ship. The soldier reported the incident, but somewhere along the line, the report was lost. Just yesterday the report was refiled."

"So our traitor is somewhere along that chain of command," Ladan said, spooning ginter into a glass pot.

"Or at the top. The report eventually goes to Joakim. And Joakim's secretary handles everything he sees."

Ladan took the boiling water from the cook-top and poured it over the tea. "Keep searching, Jeiel. I'll talk to Joakim today." He looked up and saw Talia hovering in the doorway to the sleeping chamber. He held up the pot. "Would you like some ginter tea?"

"Please," she eagerly answered.

Ladan gave Jeiel a smug look, then filled two cups.

Jeiel did not accompany Ladan and Talia to the trading market, explaining to Talia he knew nothing of female clothing and could be of little use. As Ladan and Talia rode in the TC, Talia's curiosity won out over her tangled emotions, and she enjoyed the trip to the center of the city and the main market. Eagerly, she watched the sights of the gleaming city zip by. The streets were clean, lined with trees and flowers. A mixture of many races, dressed in different costumes, strolled on the sidewalks and crowded the main market square.

"Why are the merchants divided in the manner they are?" Talia asked, after disembarking the TC and glancing down the street of food sellers.

"What do you mean?" Ladan absently asked, surveying the area.

"All the dealers of a particular item have their own street. Why do they not mix?"

"Such as having a jeweler next to a glass blower?"

Talia smiled, pleased he had understood her question. "Exactly."

"I have never thought about it. I guess it comes from tradition. When traders first came to Gemmal, there were many dishonest ones, and the Geala stopped buying. The merchants, in order to protect themselves, set up trade unions and sanctioned each new member, then gave that new member space on their street. If the Geala bought from merchants on the trade streets, they knew the seller was honest."

"They were resourceful people, those merchants."

"They were greedy men who didn't want their profits spoiled by a few bad men."

Talia stopped in the midst of the congested street and stared at Ladan. "Do you never see the good in others?"

"I've only been treated to the worst in most. I've seen little good."

The joy of the moment shattered, Talia glanced away from Ladan's piercing eyes.

You are the bastard Jeiel claims you are, Ladan harshly thought, looking at Talia's bent head. Why had he deliberately destroyed her joy and excitement? Instead of taunting her, he should try to see the world though her eyes, where experiences were new and untarnished. Although he discerned the evil in people and warily watched them, that didn't mean he had to taint Talia's views of others. That would come from experience itself.

He grabbed her hand and led her to a shop where a man was blowing glass.

"Look, Talia," he softly commanded, pointing to the worker.

She followed his finger. Her eyes widened with wonder and delight at the man's skill.

"The first time I saw a glass blower I had just arrived on the planet of Trifid from Darka. As I wandered through the market area, I saw a man handling the hot glass. I spent hours watching him work. It seemed like magic to me how he could blow through that long tube and fashion a thing of fragile beauty. The shopkeeper noticed me and guessed my plight and offered me a job. I swept his store and ran errands for him. He was a kind man who took in strays like me. One of his strays killed him for a gold coin. A lousy payment for a good act."

Talia allowed Ladan several moments to grieve for his friend, then held out her hand. "Where are the clothing merchants?"

"On the next street."

Ladan held firmly to Talia's hand, after she had stopped unexpectedly several times to gaze into shop windows and he had walked on without her. Aware of the danger to her with the traitor still loose, Ladan closely watched anyone who approach her.

After visiting four clothing shops and disliking their stock, Ladan pulled Talia into a small building tucked between two powerful merchants. Here, he found the items he wanted. After purchasing a robe and several gowns that were to be worn to bed, Talia whispered in his ear that she wished to buy several articles of clothing of a personal nature. Ladan quietly exited and stood outside the shop.

"Ladan," a husky female voice called.

Jerking around, Ladan came face to face with a tall, well-endowed female with midnight black hair and hot red nails. Her white, perfumed hand slipped inside his vest to caress his bare chest as she raised up on her toes and kissed his lips.

"I heard you were back. Why have you not come to see me?"

"He has been busy," Talia coldly answer.

Talia's answer stunned him. One glance over his shoulder confirmed that Talia was embarrassed by her rudeness, but she held her head high in spite of her pink cheeks.

"Who is this pale creature, Ladan?" the buxom female asked.

Ladan stretched his neck and cleared his throat, uncomfortable with the situation. "Ola, this is Talia."

Is that all you have to say? Talia silently asked Ladan.

"My mate," he finished.

"What?" came Ola's strangled reply. Her eyes narrowed as she studied Talia from head to toe. Ladan's medallion dangled on Talia's forehead, making Ola frown when she saw it. Quickly she looked back at Ladan, noticing for the first time he wore only one armband. "Show her the matching band, Talia."

Talia slid up the sleeve of her coat-dress.

Ola shook her head. Her eyes were overbright when she addressed Ladan. "I never thought you would take a wife. Your heart is too hard to give a female what she needs." She whirled, charging blindly into the crowd.

"Who was she, Ladan?"

"A paid-woman, Talia. Do you understand what that terms means?" When she remained silent, he said, "I didn't think so. Never mind. It isn't important."

As he left the market, he felt a twinge of pity for Ola. She'd always welcomed him into her bed when he returned to Gemmal, but there had always been a price. She might have cared for him, but she liked his wealth more.

Ladan stole a glance at Talia. Her back was ramrod straight as she stiffly walked to the TC.

A smile broke out on his face. His little Geala was jealous. So jealous that she could not control her tongue. The thought pleased him.

Appalled by her inexcusable rudeness and the burning jealousy that prompted her behavior, Talia withdrew into herself. She said nothing on the way back from the market, and once inside Ladan's house, she walked into the bed chamber and sat down on the bed, staring blindly at the white wall.

How could she have acted so shockingly? What was wrong with her character that she could not control herself? It must be an awful flaw to experience such hot envy. As she thought back to the instant she saw other female touch Ladan, the heated reaction of wanting to smack away the other woman's arms surfaced, again.

She wrapped her shaking arms around her waist. What was happening to her? The seams of her life were unraveling, leaving the fabric of her existence unrecognizable.

In the next room, Ladan felt Talia's turmoil. He cursed her strict Geala upbringing that valued politeness above everything, no matter what the sacrifice. He'd seen that pattern in his mother. She was always unfailingly polite, even after his father had beaten her.

He entered the dark room and turned on the overhead light. Talia did not move. He knelt before her and clasped her left hand between his.

"Jealousy is a normal emotion, Talia. It's a common

thread among all races. I think even the Geala experienced it."

Her eyes locked with his, and he saw she doubted his last statement. He shrugged. "Well, I suppose they did. How could anyone tell, when they never showed any emotion at all?"

"What I did was unforgivable."

"Who will care and count it against you? Me? Ola? The people passing by?"

"I care, Ladan. I was raised with certain rules and values, and what I did, giving into my jealousy and being rude, broke those rules. My actions are an anathema to my kind. To me."

Hot rage thundered though him. She was going to kill herself with those rules. Grasping her arms, he brought her face close to his. "Oh, yes, Talia, hold it in. Never show any emotion, even if it twists your soul, slowly killing you. Die inside, but always be polite."

"You do not understand," she brokenly whispered.

"No, it's you who doesn't understand. You're a tasha trying to behave as a full-blooded Geala. You cannot be something you're not."

All color fled her face, leaving her dark blue eyes even more vivid against her pale features. Her pain—the pain he caused—hit him full force, wrenching his heart. His hands slid up to cup her face. "My tenata, you are half Alcoran. To deny that half of you is wrong and will leave you incomplete."

The door chime sounded. Ladan reluctantly stood and left the room. He saw Jeiel through the side panel by the door.

"Forgive the interruption," Jeiel said. "Joakim wishes to see you."

"Have you discovered anything new?" Ladan asked, glancing at the bed chamber door.

Jeiel shook his head. "No. Joakim suspects a traitor, but I didn't confirm his suspicions or tell him about the missing report. I thought perhaps you would want that honor."

"You are almost as good as Talia at reading my mind."

"It comes from years of experience," Jeiel responded.

"Will you stay here with Talia?" Ladan asked. "You're the only one I trust to keep her safe."

"That's why I'm here."

"It's a debt I'll never be able to repay, but I'll try."

"Perhaps one day our roles will be reversed."

Ladan wanted to go back into the other room and ease Talia's pain and confusion, but he realized she needed time to deal with her emotions. With a heavy sigh, he left.

Jeiel walked around the main room waiting for Talia to appear. Finally, he gave up and called her.

"Talia, would you like for me to fix you some tea?"

When she emerged from the bed chamber, she appeared pale and shaken.

"Talia, what's wrong?" Jeiel asked, moving to her side. He reached for her, but she shook away his offer of help.

"I believe some ginter tea would help."

Jeiel grimaced. "That bad?"

Talia walked to the cooking room and gathered the things for tea. As she did so, she asked, "Who is Ola?"

He whistled and shook his hand. "How do you know about Ola?"

"She poured herself all over Ladan when we were in the market."

The twitching of his lips was Jeiel's only reaction. Talia

felt her cheeks redden again at her outward manifestation of jealousy. It was an ugly emotion, one which she detested but seemed to have no control over.

Seeing her distress, Jeiel's amusement fled. "Ola is no one to worry about, Talia. Ladan simply enjoyed her company while here in Ezion Geber. There have been many different females over the years that Ladan has known. None were special."

Talia dropped the metal pot of boiling water back on the cook-top, then covered her face with her hands.

"No, Talia, no," he said, hurrying to her. "I did not mean you were included. Somehow, Ladan is different with you. Never before has he claimed a female as his own. Ola is a paid-woman. Any male who has enough coin can lay with her. Ladan never cared for any of those females beyond the easing of his body. With you, he becomes someone I have trouble recognizing. I never knew who his parents were before this last trip. When he told me, I nearly fainted from surprise. And knowing Ladan has telepathic ability is a chilling thought." He cocked his head and stared at Talia. "That's what it is, Talia. There's some deep, mystic bond between you and Ladan that never existed for him with any other female."

A throbbing started behind her eyes, making it hard to think. "I am very tired. Perhaps I should rest before the fete tonight."

As she walked by him, Jeiel touched her arm. "Talia, don't worry. Ladan recognizes the bond between you."

Talia's lips turned up, but it was not a smile. "My question, Jeiel, is whether the bond he feels is the same as the one I feel? Or is fidelity missing from his? Can you answer me that?"

"No. I doubt even Ladan could answer you honestly at this point."

"It is as I thought."

Her last thought before she slipped from consciousness was that pain now had a new meaning.

Chapter 14

Ladan barged into Joakim's office, past the startled Artis.

"You can't go in there," the assistant protested.

Ladan stopped and looked over his shoulder. "Says who?"

"Uh ... well—"

"Are you planning to stop me?" Ladan asked in a low, deadly voice.

Artis shook his head. Nodding, Ladan turned and threw opened the heavy door. Joakim glanced up.

"Ladan, what can I do for you? Did I forget an appointment we had?"

Ladan didn't bother to answer. He simply grabbed the older man's arm and pulled him to his feet.

"What do you think you are doing?" Joakim sputtered.

"Come with me, old man. We have something to discuss."

"How dare you?" Joakim huffed as he stumbled along beside Ladan.

Once in the hall, a soldier approached the duo. "First Secretary, is something wrong?" the young private asked.

Ladan paused and looked meaningfully at Joakim. Apparently, the older man must have received the warning in Ladan's eyes because Joakim waved the soldier away.

"No, everything is fine. Go back to your post."

"That was very wise of you," Ladan whispered as they walked out of the building. Once they were clear of the doorway, Joakim pulled away and stopped.

"I assume you have a good reason for your actions. What you've done could be considered—"

"What?" Ladan asked, his fierce expression making Joakim take a step back.

"Unwise."

"What is unwise, Joakim, is to harbor a traitor at the highest level of the Alliance."

"Are you calling me a traitor?" Joakim asked, indignation flushing his face.

"No. I don't doubt your loyalty. It is those around you who I suspect are helping the Dyne."

"What proof do you have that there is a traitor?"

"Aside from the fact that the Dyne knew every move I made when I was searching for Toaeth and sent assassins at every turn. And what of the attempted poisoning of all the Alliance ambassadors?"

Joakim refused to meet Ladan's eyes.

"What leads me to suspect someone in your office was an incident with a cargo vessel that occurred several weeks ago and the report on it that appeared in your office only yesterday. Someone buried that report to hide the illegal transmission and the disappearance of the ship. Now why would someone what to do that?"

"It could be just a natural slip up," Joakim offered lamely.

"No, Joakim. There's a traitor within your inner circle. Do you have any idea who it might be?"

Folding his arms over his chest, Joakim stroked his chin. "There are only two men who knew about your mission. Artis, my assistant, and Milon, the commander of the combined forces. But Artis has been with me since I was elected First Secretary, and Milon . . ." Joakim rubbed his neck. "Perhaps there is some kind of listening device in my office and someone else is behind these leaks."

The old man wanted to take the easy way out and blame others than his closest associates, but he would soon find out he couldn't hide from the truth. Ladan wouldn't let him. "Have your office checked, but I doubt you'll find anything. I'll give you this warning, First Secretary, you better find that bastard before I do, because if I get to him first, I'll cut his heart out."

Ladan didn't like the worried expression on Jeiel's face when he walked into his house. "Where's Talia?"

"Resting. The encounter with Ola upset her."

Ladan sprawled out on the long, low couch. "Talia was jealous. Jealousy isn't a prized emotion among the Geala."

"It's more than that, Ladan. I think for the first time she realizes that perhaps you do not look upon your commitment to the marriage as she does."

Ladan sat up, pinning Jeiel with a hard look. "What do you mean?"

"Fidelity. She asked about it."

Ladan cursed soundly. "There's a traitor running loose, trying to murder all the leaders of the Alliance, Talia's at risk from the same source, we've a missing cargo vessel, probably filled with Dyne assassins, and my little Geala is worried about my hormones." He laughed bitterly. "What a mess."

"You need to talk to her."

"I know."

Ladan watched Jeiel leave. He rubbed the back of his neck. Things should've quieted down. Instead, they were escalating out of control. With a sigh, he rose and moved to the bed chamber. It took several moments for his eyes to adjust to the darkness of the room. Talia was curled on her side, asleep on the bed. What an innocent she had been when he plucked her off Petar. Now . . .

She was still innocent in so many ways. Somehow, he would have to help Talia face and deal with the unfamiliar emotions of her Alcoran half. Perhaps that way she would finally find peace with herself.

He sat down and lightly stroked her cheek. "Little Geala, wake up."

She moaned and turned her face into the soft mattress. Her reaction alerted him. Ladan slipped his hand under her neck, and he turned her face up to him. "Talia, what's wrong?"

"My head," she mumbled. "It hurts."

Panic seized him. "I'll find a physician."

She grasped his arm. "No. Perhaps with a bit more sleep the pain will disappear."

Ladan wasn't pleased with her suggestion, but he yielded, wanting to give her the thing she wanted. He stretched out beside her and gathered her into his arms.

"What are you doing?" she sleepily asked, snuggling closer.

"Giving in to the desire to hold you." His fingers gently rubbed her temples and brow. "Go to sleep, my tenata. I'm here."

Ladan pulled Talia across the room and gently pushed her out of the house.

"What are you doing?" she asked, surprised by Ladan's actions.

"Taking you to see someone you should have seen the first day you were here." While she had slept, Ladan determined the best way for Talia to deal with her Alcoran heritage was to learn about it.

Talia sat quietly in the TC.

"Stop that," Ladan softly commanded, taking hold of her hand.

"Stop what?"

"Trying to read my mind. You'll find out soon enough where we're going. Look out over the city. Isn't the pattern of lights beautiful? Or if that does not interest you, look up at the sky. Do you see the shifting green and red lights, shining like a curtain? The aurora borealis. I bet you could tell me what causes that phenomenon."

"Auroras are produced by electrical charges in the upper atmosphere that cause the air to glow. The charge comes from particles the planet's star sends out. The phenomenon can occur at any time, but is more likely to occur when the star is very active, producing large numbers of solar spots."

Ladan grinned. "I knew you would know."

"Now, where are we going?"

The TC stopped and the doors slid open. "We're

going to see some of your relatives." Seeing the look of terror in Talia's eyes, Ladan grabbed her hand.

Ladan stopped before a large, white building. The enormous carved doors were flooded with lights. Talia pulled back.

"Why are you doing this?" she asked, her voice quivering.

"Because you need to face the truth. If you know about your mother's people, Talia, then, can you understand yourself."

He was right. Only by knowing that heritage could she deal with all the unruly thoughts and feelings that tore her apart. Lifting her chin, she met his gaze. "I am ready."

Ladan's knock was immediately answered, and they were led to a small salon with several couches and chairs. An elderly man, with flowing silver hair and beard, sat in a special chair on wheels. A younger man, about Talia's age, stood behind him. The last man, somewhere in age between the other two, was seated on the couch.

"Ladan," the man on the couch exclaimed as he stood. He shook Ladan's hand, then turned to Talia. He studied her for a moment before leaning down and kissing Talia's cheek.

Startled, Talia jerked back.

The man looked questioningly at Ladan.

"Talia was raised as a Geala. She doesn't comprehend your method of greeting."

Both Talia and the man shifted. The uncomfortable silence broke when the old man spoke.

"Come here, daughter of my dearest niece."

Talia moved to stand in front of the crippled man. Slowly his eyes roamed over her. When his gaze met hers, Talia looked into eyes as blue as her own. She recognized him. He was family.

A welcoming smile spread across the man's tired features. "I see your mother in you. I'm glad she left such a lovely legacy. I am Aram, a distant cousin of your mother's father. This"—he pointed over his shoulder—"is my grandson, Noan, and his father, Seath. I have been ill, or I would have demanded to see you the instant it was announced who you were."

Ladan stepped to Talia's side. "Aram, Talia knows nothing of the Alcoran race. Her mother died when she was young. She didn't know what the tattoo on her forehead meant until I told her. Her father, Toaeth, told her nothing of her mother's race. She needs to know."

Aram steepled his hands and brought them up to his chin. "A child of a Geala father and Alcoran mother. An impossible mix. It's a wonder the female is sane." He glanced at Ladan.

"That's why we're here. Talia needs to understand the polarized emotions tearing her apart."

Aram motioned for them to sit. He looked deep into Talia's eyes. "Alcorans are called the warrior race. We evolved from seven tribes that roamed our planet. Then one great leader, Motis, united the tribes, and the energy we used to fight one another was turned to building. Our civilization flourished, our technology increased, and when the Dyne came, introducing their space technology, we learned from them, then fought to rid ourselves of their harsh rule. Even though we had ceased fighting among ourselves for ten generations, the warrior instinct was still there. Only this time we fought with lasers and space vessels on a broader field, with higher stakes and greater destruction."

Talia sat silently on the couch.

"Have you no questions, Talia?"

How did one ask what emotions ruled the Alcoran heart? Or what rules guided their behavior?

"Do not be shy, daughter. If you wish information, ask."

"Tell me of your social structure. What trait is most valued among your people?"

"Freedom and honor are highly prized. A man's word is his bond. To offer your home to a friend or to serve him is considered a thing of honor. We are not as stiff and formal as the Geala, but we believe in graciousness."

The young man stepped around his grandfather's chair to stand beside the couch. "You will also find that we enjoy our senses and emotions in a fuller way than the Geala. We laugh and cry. Love and hate. And although polite with others, we are open and honest with members of our immediate family."

A small frown gathered Talia's brow. "I do not know if I understand."

"Perhaps you should spend time with us," Noan responded, his blue eyes full of admiration.

Ladan stood, his expression dark, warning the young man not to trespass. "Thank you for the offer. We will consider your offer and contact you again."

Ladan clamped his hand around Talia's wrist and pulled her from the room. Shortly thereafter, as they left the house, Ladan wasn't sure he had done the right thing.

Talia felt Ladan's seething anger. She glanced at him seated on the couch across the room. "Why are you upset?"

Ladan looked up from the glass of liquor in his hands. "What makes you think I am 'upset'?"

"I can feel your indignation."

A harsh laugh escaped Ladan's mouth. "Indignation? Yeah, that's what I was feeling tonight—indignation."

Talia walked to the sofa and sat beside him. "I do not understand. Have I done something that displeases you?"

Ladan stared at the glass in his hands. "No."

"Then what is creating this storm in you?"

"It was the manner in which that young pup slobbered all over you?"

"Are you talking about Noan?"

"Yes. Did you not see the lust in his eyes?"

"No, I did not notice."

"I don't doubt that, but it was there. He thought you were beautiful and wanted you."

Heat flushed Talia's cheeks. "And now you regret taking me to see these men?"

He silently considered the question, then down the liquor in the glass. "No, I don't regret my actions. You need to know about your Alcoran heritage." His hand cupped the side of her face and his mouth covered hers in a kissing that was both a brand and a reassurance.

The uncontrollable passion that Ladan always called forth in her bubbled to the surface and she slipped her arms around his neck and kissed him back.

He raised his head and the corner of his mouth turned up. "That has almost soothed my *indignation*. But—" he ran his thumb over her lips "—I think I will require more than a few kisses."

"And what would that be?"

"Let me show you," he whispered, then picked her up and carried her into the bedroom.

* * *

The market was unusually crowded. Jeiel shoved aside the male in front of him, making a path for Talia.

"Ladan will cut me up into little pieces if anything happens to you," he threw over his shoulder at her. "I shouldn't have listened to you. You have no business in this crowded market until we know more about who the traitor is."

He stopped in front of the glassmaker's shop. "Is this the one?"

Talia glanced in the window and saw the magnificent clear blue sculpture. "Yes." She moved into the shop, leaving Jeiel to follow. Clutching her gold circlet, she approached the proprietor.

"I wish to purchase the blue sculpture you have on display in the window."

The muscular, middle-aged man smiled. "I see you are a female of rare taste." He retrieved the work and set it on a long wooden counter. "As you can see, the workmanship is of the highest quality. If you look into the center, you can see the variegated shades of blue, from indigo to azure as they swirl outward. Waves of the sea, captured in glass."

Talia laid her circlet on the counter and picked up the glass, turning it in her hands, studying it from different angles. The strength rising from the base in various hues and the awesome beauty of the piece reminded her of Ladan. This morning, when she awakened, the desire to give him something in return for the gift of knowledge he'd given her about herself by taking her to the Alcoran ambassador had overwhelmed her. The sculpture had come to mind. She had seen it yesterday when she was shopping with Ladan and knew he would like it.

"I wish to buy this. I have no coins or credit, but I thought perhaps we could barter. My circlet is gold, and I hope enough to cover the cost of the sculpture."

"No, Talia," Jeiel spoke, coming to her side. "Ladan has enough credits to cover the price of the object."

Solemnly, she turned to him. "I do not want Ladan to pay for his own gift."

"As his mate, you are entitled to his wealth."

"A gift that is not given of my sacrifice is no gift at all."

"Then charge it to Joakim. Your service to the Alliance should be rewarded."

"None was offered. None should be given for doing my duty," Talia quietly replied.

Jeiel threw up his hands in exasperation.

The shopkeeper's eyes were wide as he looked at Talia. "My lady, if you are Ladan's wife, there would be no problem purchasing the piece."

"I will not use Ladan's credit. If you will not take the circlet in trade, then I will not be able to buy the piece."

Jeiel's curse caused Talia to smile. "That must be a popular phrase with bounty hunters. I have heard Ladan use it often."

"I don't doubt it," Jeiel grumbled. He pulled on one of his braids, then scratched his beard. "How about this. I will buy the circlet and pay you, Talia—" he glanced at the owner. "How much is the work worth?"

"50 credits."

Jeiel's eyes narrowed. "How much?"

"Well, for this lovely female, the heroine who saved the Alliance, 38 credits."

Nodding his approval, Jeiel turned back to Talia. "I will pay you 50 credits."

The shopkeeper choked. "B—but—"

"That way," Jeiel continued ruthlessly, "you will have some extra credits to purchase other items."

Her eyes shimmering with moisture, Talia whispered her thanks.

After the transaction was keyed into the main computer, the owner carefully wrapped the sculpture. As Talia watched him, the nagging pain that had been behind her eyes sharpened. She gasped and glanced around the shop. It was as if someone were aiming beam at her head, shredding her skull into a million pieces.

"Talia, what's wrong?" Jeiel asked.

The pain became worse. Her field of vision darkened, and black spots appeared before her eyes. She swayed.

Jeiel scooped her up before she fell. "What is it?"

"My head. It hurts."

"I'll take you home. I just hope Ladan gives me time to explain before he slices me in two." He started for the door.

"Wait," she weakly cried. "The sculpture."

He turned, and the owner placed the piece in Talia's hands.

"Thank you," she whispered, resting her head on Jeiel's shoulder.

The trip back to Ladan's house was a blur, but she knew the moment they arrived home because she could hear Ladan bellowing.

"Where have you been? I came home—what happened? If she's hurt, I'll kill you."

"Shame on you, Ladan," Talia softly reprimanded her husband as she felt him take her from Jeiel's arms.

"Jeiel was kind enough to accompany me to the market."

Ladan snorted. "What happened?"

"I'm not sure. Her head started hurting, then she collapsed."

Ladan laid her on the bed, then tried to take the package from her. She refused to release it. Ladan knelt at her side.

"What is it you risked your life to buy? Haven't I provided everything you needed?"

"You have provided more than enough. I wanted to give you a gift." She placed the wrapped piece in his hands.

Ladan went still. Never had he received a gift. He glanced up and saw Jeiel in the doorway, his friend's eyes condemning him for his last comment. His palms sweating, Ladan unwrapped the gift. His hands hovered above the swirling blue glass. He gulped hard as he carefully picked up the sculpture.

Talia watched through pain-glazed eyes as Ladan studied the work from several different angles. "It was you in crystal. I wished for you to have it."

Ladan's chest tightened. Raw power captured in blue. It was magnificent. And he suddenly realized she saw him in that light. He grasped her left hand and placed a kiss on the blue star. "Thank you."

Talia's eyes fluttered closed, and she sighed in contentment. Ladan stood and, with the sculpture in his hand, went into the main room.

"She didn't use any of your credits to purchase it. Instead, she tried to barter her circlet for it." Jeiel held out the gold band. "I bought it."

"I want to buy it back."

"I knew you would." Jeiel handed Ladan the gold band.

Ladan slumped down on the couch. He looked from the circlet to the gleaming work. "I will have to summon a physician for her. There's something wrong."

"I know of a Mizan doctor who has treated several Alcoran officials."

"Good. Bring him." Ladan heard Jeiel leave, but he didn't move. Within his hands he held Talia's love. It was a stunning revelation to a man who thought love would never touch his life.

"What's wrong with her?"

Ladan's expression made the doctor wince.

"I can find no physical origin for the headaches."

"What the hell is that supposed to mean?" Ladan growled.

"It means there is an outside reason for the pain."

"Explain."

"I mean that there is no tumor or physical reason within the female to cause her pain."

"So?"

"That leaves an outside source. Poison could cause the reaction, or perhaps something in the air or something she consumed that is contaminating her system."

"That makes no sense. This was the home planet of the Geala," Jeiel interjected, entering the conversation for the first time.

The doctor turned to him. "Many changes have occurred in the atmosphere since the Geala lived here. Pollutants, new foods from different parts of the star system. Any number of things." He looked at Ladan. "You will need to observe the pattern of the headaches.

If they happen after she has eaten or had something to drink, then it might be poisoned."

"Would the poison produce the same result in me?" Ladan asked.

"It depends on your heritage. I will take a blood sample and test it for known poisons."

Ladan glanced at Jeiel. "Can you give her anything to ease the pain?"

"Yes."

"Good. I will not see her suffer."

The next few days pushed Talia to the limit. Her headaches increased in length and intensity. They came at no regular intervals nor after she had consumed a particular food or drink, but were random, occurring both day and night.

Beside the onslaught of headaches, the round of receptions and fetes also drained Talia. It seemed that each ambassador wanted to out-do the others in the lavishness of the party he threw to honor her. All assumed she would take her proper place as a royal princess, working for the Alliance.

The leaders wanted Talia to take her mother's place. They wanted her to be her mother, but she could not. What did she know about being a royal princess? She was raised in isolation, as a Geala to pursue knowledge, to work in harmony with her surroundings, to be fruitful and modest. And although her thirst for knowledge and her curiosity about the new things around her had not died, she knew that she could not endure a lifetime here in Ezion Geber. Yet, didn't she have a responsibility to her mother's people?

Talia observed that Ladan was not welcome among

the elite of the Alliance. They said nothing disparaging to his face, but Talia read in their actions and eyes the wariness and disdain they held for her husband. And although Ladan would never admit it, the snubs wounded him.

The night of the Alcoran reception was pleasantly warm, fragrant with the perfume of the flowers blooming throughout the city. The ambassador had sent Talia a traditional Alcoran costume earlier in the day, and she had dressed in the flowing white gown, trimmed with gold thread around the neck, bell-sleeves and skirt hem. A wide golden sash finished the outfit.

As soon as they arrived, Noan had attached himself to Talia, introducing her to the guests. They politely greeted Ladan, but after the initial greeting, had ignored him, concentrating on her.

Ladan sipped the Mythinan brandy and scanned the room, looking for the two prime suspects in order to take his mind off the slobbering Alcoran youth who was talking to Talia.

When his eyes came back to Talia, he cursed soundly. This was the fourth reception in as many days. He didn't need any telepathic ability to know the strain she was under. Any fool could tell from her tight expression and stiff movements she was pulled so taut that at any moment she might snap under the tension.

Suddenly, his skin prickled and his hunting instincts roared a warning. Talia. She was in danger. He turned and saw her rubbing her temples, then she shook her head as if to clear it.

Before he could move, he heard Talia's strangled cry, followed by Noan's shout. Talia dug the heels of her hands into the upper ridge of her eye sockets, as if to hold her head together. She swayed, then fell to her knees.

Ladan darted to her side, knelt, and wrapped his arms around her.

"Make it stop," she moaned. "Make the pain in my head stop."

Ladan felt the searing pain, like flames licking the inside of his skull. Glancing at Noan he asked, "Did she have anything to eat or drink?"

"No," Talia groaned. "Telepathically. The pain is being sent to me from another source." She hunched further into herself. "I cannot stand it," she brokenly cried.

Ladan shot to his feet and scanned the room. His eyes stopped on a strange man wearing a hooded cloak, standing close to a tall plant. The moment Ladan's eyes met his, the man began to back toward the door.

"Stop," Ladan thundered.

The man paid no heed, but whirled and ran for the door. Automatically, Ladan pulled his knife and threw it. His aim was true, hitting the man middle of the back. The stranger fell dead just inside the open portal.

Talia gasped and went limp, sprawling on the floor. Ladan didn't bother with the dead man. Instead, he knelt beside Talia and gathered her up in his arms.

Jeiel pushed through the people crowded around the body. With his foot, Jeiel rolled the cloaked figured onto his side. The concealing hood fell back to reveal an orange-haired man with a blue tattoo that covered part of his right jaw and throat.

"A Gimitian," Jeiel announced.

The crowd gasped.

"And the only other telepathic race in the star system," Ladan ground out. "Menoth wants his revenge on Talia."

"But how did a Gimitian, a member of Dyne Union, get here?" asked the Alcoran ambassador.

Ladan and Jeiel exchanged a meaningful glance. The missing cargo vessel held the answer.

"A question that I will find the answer to," Ladan solemnly vowed before walking out of the reception, Talia cradled in his arms.

Ladan sat on the bed beside Talia. The doctor had left after giving her a sedative. He had pronounced her unharmed physically from the attack.

"I've read where the Dyne used Gimitians to cause the Geala pain, thus controlling them," Jeiel said.

"Why didn't we think of that before?" Ladan's fingers combed through Talia's hair.

"Who'd ever think that a Gimitian could slip unnoticed onto Gemmal?"

Ladan's eyes narrowed. "We need to find that cargo vessel and see if there are any others who accompanied the Gimitian."

"I did hear an interesting rumor this afternoon in a bar on the outskirts of the city. Several of the males were talking that there was more than one person involved in the plan to kill the ambassadors. The incident tonight rather confirms that rumor."

"I know Menoth has put a price on Talia's head. Until we know what we are fighting, she cannot be left alone. Will you help me guard her?"

Jeiel nodded. "I have a friend in the military I trust. He owes me a favor, so I plan to ask him to use the low level satellite to scan the planet's surface for our missing vessel. If I don't turn up anything, then I take out a low-flying ship and search until we find some sign of it."

Ladan pressed the bridge of his nose with his thumb and forefinger. "We can take turns searching."

Jeiel's clear green eyes held Ladan's. "We'll find them."

"You're right."

When he was alone, Ladan leaned down and softly kissed Talia's lips. "Menoth will not harm you, my tenata. Not while I draw breath."

Chapter 15

The warmth beside her reassured Talia. She was safe. Her eyes fluttered open to encounter Ladan's concerned gaze.

His hand cupped her cheek. "How are you feeling?"

"I am well."

He drew her close, tucking her head under his chin. "I wish it was me, Talia, they wanted. It would be easier to endure. You must realize Menoth wants you dead, even through we outmaneuvered him and defeated his forces, he still wants his revenge. But don't worry, *my tenata*, Jeiel and I will be with you until we catch the traitor."

Talia was never left alone after that morning. Ladan and Jeiel took turns guarding her, while the other flew reconnaissance missions over the planet, searching for some sign of the missing cargo ship. On the third day, Ladan spotted the ship hidden between two tall peaks a hundred kilometers from Ezion Geber.

He landed his craft in a small clearing on the far side of one of the peaks and hiked around the base of the mountain. He cautiously approached the quiet vessel, in spite of feeling that the ship was deserted. His instincts were correct; the ship was empty. From the condition of the main cabin, Ladan guessed that there had been more than one person hiding within the hull of the vessel.

He carefully searched the rest of the craft, inspecting each storage-hold. When he was satisfied no one was hiding among the cargo, he left.

Once back in the city, Ladan went directly to Joakim's office, intending to learn to whom the ship was registered and who had been her captain. The moment he entered Joakim's office, he knew something major had happened.

"Ladan, good news." Joakim rose from his desk and hurried around it. "General Treay has defeated the remaining Dyne force near the planet of Usol. Their fleet was completely destroyed. The Dyne Union will never rise again." Joakim shook his head. "If it had not been for Talia raising the shields, we never would have been able to put such a large force into the fight against the Dyne." He paced before his desk. "What a victory! What a victory!"

Something about the situation didn't sit right with Ladan. "What about Menoth?"

"Ah, yes, the mighty Menoth. General Treay said Menoth's ship was blown up. With no ships and no leader, the Union is dead. I never thought I'd see this day. Peace."

The news of his father's death should've brought some sort of satisfaction or relief. It didn't. There was no easing of the knot of hatred in the center of Ladan's chest. "What are you planning to do with the other members of the Union? Do you intend to rule them militarily? Or will you permit them to join the Alliance? Or do you intent to ignore them and go about your business?"

"I don't know. I don't think anyone thought beyond saving the Alliance. We'll have to have a council meeting and decide our course. But tonight we celebrate, and I'd be honored if you and Talia would join me and the other leaders in our rejoicing."

"Of course. Where else would Talia be but among the elite of the Alliance on such an auspicious occasion?"

Joakim frowned, and Ladan stiffened, annoyed that he had revealed his jealousy.

"Talia and I will be there." He turned and headed for the door.

"Ladan, what brought you here? It wasn't news of our victory."

Joakim's question stopped him. "I found the missing cargo vessel. What I want to know was who was the captain of the *Dealia* and what was her registry?"

"I'll find out. Did you discover anything else?"

"No, but I have the feeling there's another assassin just waiting for the right moment."

"Who do you think his target will be?"

"Talia."

The streets of the taciturn city of Ezion Geber were crowded with exuberant, rejoicing citizens. Ladan stopped and watched the normally dignified people shout for joy and hug any stranger who would hug them back. Among that happy throng was an assassin. He could feel it. The danger had not passed.

HUNTER'S HEART

* * *

The loud crowd grated on Ladan's nerves. Everyone at the fete wanted to hover around Talia, hailing her as the savior of the Alliance. He'd bet General Treay would have a different view on the subject.

He gulped down another healthy swig of brandy, then headed toward the bar for a refill. Once he had another drink, he turned and glared at the youth at Talia's side.

"If you don't stop glaring, you're going to burn a hole in that boy," Jeiel casually said as he stopped by Ladan's side.

"If that boy doesn't keep his hands to himself, he'll not live to see another birthday."

Jeiel nodded in understanding. "Just don't let anyone see you when you dispose of the body. It would end your brilliant career within the Alliance."

"Ah, hell, Jeiel, she belongs with them, not with me." Ladan turned away from his friend's penetrating stare.

"You are right, Ladan. Talia and the Alcoran youth make a handsome couple."

Ladan faced Jeiel, his eyes filled with burning fires.

"Self-doubt and pity have never been your companions," Jeiel chided. "Why now?"

"Because she deserves more than the meanest bastard in the star system. I will crush her if she stays with me."

"No, Ladan. You will crush her if you leave her or force her away. Either way, you will rob her of her heart. She will be as incomplete as you."

"You're wrong. She's a princess and belongs among these aristocrats."

"You're a fool."

"No, just a realist."

* * *

Talia knew something was wrong. She had sensed Ladan's disquiet all evening. He had said nothing verbally to her since they left the celebration. His mind was clouded with dark emotions, and he had turned from her so she could not read his mind.

She waited until they were safely home before she spoke. Reaching out, she lightly touched his arm. "Ladan?"

He stared down at the delicate hand resting on his forearm. His eyes traveled up her arm, over the soft shoulder to the anxious indigo eyes watching him.

"Aren't you frightened to touch me, when all those tonight shivered when my eyes even rested on them?"

"No."

He grasped her upper arms with punishing strength and hauled her close. "Why? You're an intelligent female, why do you have no fear of me?"

"You are my mate, Ladan, the one who has held me when I was frightened, taught me of the new universe I entered, kept me safe, walked with me through the darkness. How can I fear you after all we have endured together?"

"But you are a princess."

Her eyes darkened with turmoil, and Ladan was alerted to her distress, but before he could kiss her to divert her thoughts, Talia leaned up and covered his lips with hers. When her small tongue slipped into his mouth, Ladan stumbled toward the couch, his hands making quick work of their clothing. Never before had Talia initiated their joining. A guilty Ladan basked in the knowledge that his little reserved Geala physically wanted him. It was a rare joy that he held in his heart as they made love.

Afterward, as she lay curled against his side, Ladan admitted to himself that he loved her. And because he loved her, he would release her. She belonged among her kind, serving the Alliance as she was meant to, and not with him. He only hoped the Geala bond that had pulled her back from madness could be weakened enough to allow her to remarry and enjoy a full life with another.

He knew he would not.

Ladan didn't know what woke him. He listened carefully but could detect no unusual sound in the room. But his instincts cried out, *intruder*. His eyes adjusted to the low light, and he slowly scanned the room. By the door he detected a darker shadow. He slid his hand under his pillow and grasped the knife he always slept with.

As the shadow shifted, Ladan threw the anlace. The laser in the assailant's hand fired as the figure fell to the floor. Ladan dove, taking Talia with him over the far side of the bed away from the attacker.

"What is it?" Talia whispered.

"Stay here," Ladan commanded. He crawled around the edge of the bed until he could see the still figure on the floor. With caution he approached the body. The laser gun lay several centimeters away from the assailant. Ladan scooped up the weapon, aiming it at the figure's head. With a rough kick, Ladan turned the body.

"Talia, go to the communication panel and summon

the city police. Tell them to notify Joakim that another assassin has been killed."

Once she had pulled on her robe and left the room, Ladan turned on the overhead lights. Blank eyes stared up at him. He immediately recognized a fellow bounty hunter—Gretis. And although the cargo vessel was probably registered to another, Ladan knew that Gretis had piloted the ship. Among the hardened group of bounty hunters, Gretis was considered scum.

"Ladan?"

He wanted to protect her from the ugly sight of death. She'd seen too much already. "Don't come in here, Talia. I'll dress and be there in a moment."

He emerged from the bed chamber, dressed only in his black pants. He headed for the cook area and started making ginter tea.

"Have you notified the authorities?"

Talia sat at the counter. "Yes. They will be here soon."

She said nothing else, but Ladan heard her thoughts clearly. *When will it end?*

He turned and covered her hand with his. "Soon, little Geala. Soon all this terror will come to an end."

Her lips quivered and her eyes filled with tears. "The water is boiling," she said in a throaty voice, trying to maintain her control.

Ladan quickly made the tea, then ushered her to the cream-colored couch. They drank the brew in companionable silence. The chime from the door caused her to jump. Ladan kissed her quickly, then answered the door.

Joakim, flanked by four city men, rushed in. The First Secretary looked less than dignified, with his nightwear tucked into his pants and his hair flying wildly about his face.

"Show me where," Joakim demanded, forgoing the usual greeting.

Ladan calmly led Joakim to the body.

The First Secretary growled a curse. "Dead. Again. You know, Ladan, it would help this investigation immensely if you left one of the suspects alive to question."

Ladan shrugged. "He left me no choice. It was either him or me. I don't kill for the pleasure of it."

Joakim blanched, and Ladan was satisfied the First Secretary understood he was displeased with the criticism.

Cocking his head, Joakim looked at the assailant. "Do I know that man?"

"I doubt you've had dealings with him, but you've probably seen him in the city. Gretis is—was—a bounty hunter. He was also scum. I don't doubt Menoth bought him, had him fly in the Grimitian. When the Grimitian failed, I'm sure Gretis was ordered to finish the job."

"Ordered by whom? We've intercepted no communications from the surface to an outside satellite."

"Your traitor, Joakim," Ladan curtly replied. His hard eyes pinned the First Secretary. "I intend to confront our two suspects and discover which one is guilty. I'll not have Talia's life endangered another day."

"When?"

"Now."

"I'm coming with you. I want to make sure I hear what they have to say before anything unfortunate happens to them."

"You're a wise man." *Wise enough to know you cannot stop me,* Ladan silently added.

Ladan kicked once. Artis's door gave way beneath the brutal assault. The apartment was a standard model for the city, and Ladan knew where every room was located. He strode in, going directly to the bed chamber.

"Wouldn't it help if we had light?" Joakim asked from the front door.

"It doesn't matter."

Joakim touched the light panel by the door, flooding the room with soft illumination. Ladan threw open the bed chamber door and lunged for the bed before Artis could move. The sleepy man gasped as he was hauled from the bed by a hand around his neck.

"Ladan," Joakim admonished. "Don't kill the man before we have a chance to question him. Allow him to talk."

Ladan threw the man back on the bed. "So talk."

Eyes wide, Artis looked from Ladan to Joakim. "What does he want me to talk about?"

"I want to know how Menoth knew my every step from the instant I left here to find the Geala to tonight when Gretis tried to kill Talia in her sleep. There were only two people who knew of my quest. You and General Milon."

"Y-you certainly don't suspect me?" Artis squeaked. "Why, what would I have to gain?"

"That's what I want to know," Ladan flung back.

"Nothing. I have no reason to betray the Alliance."

"Power, Artis, is a strong seducer. You are so close

to it, yet you wield no real power. That could make any man eager to look for a way to betray his superior in order to claim the power for himself."

Artis went white as a true Geala. "No, that's not true. I have no desire for Joakim's job. He is like a father to me." He turned to Joakim. "Isn't it true?"

Joakim stepped between Ladan and Artis. "I believe him, Ladan. I don't think he's our traitor."

Eyes never leaving the quivering man on the bed, Ladan said, "All right, we'll question General Milon. If I'm not satisfied with his answers, I'll be back to question you, Artis, again. Be here, because if you're not, I'll find you, and kill you, without asking any questions."

The trip across town to General Milon's home took precious minutes as far as Ladan was concerned. The entire time, he couldn't shake the feeling that they were pursuing a dead end. He knew it when they arrived and found the front door of the General's home open.

Joakim stared down at what was left of General Milon's body after he'd shot himself in the head with a traditional gun. He turned away and noticed the handwritten note on the desk. With trembling fingers, Joakim picked it up. After reading the suicide note, he handed it to Ladan.

"I guess that solves the mystery of who the traitor was," Joakim slowly said.

The solution was too easy. *I'm sorry*. Two words to explain a lifetime of service. It didn't make sense. Had the general been afraid that if Gretis was caught, he would identify him as the traitor? And what were his reasons for betraying his own?

Joakim called the city men, and he and Ladan waited until the police arrived.

The first rays of the day pierced the sky as Ladan walked home. He had called Jeiel to stay with Talia while he had ventured out to question the suspects. According to Joakim, everything was solved, all the loose ends tied up.

Ladan only wished that he believed it.

Chapter 16

Talia gripped the edge of the counter as a wave of nausea swamped her.

"What's wrong?" Ladan asked, coming up behind her and grasping her shoulders.

She shook her head. "Nothing. My stomach is a little unsettled. It is nothing to be alarmed about."

Poisoned. She's been poisoned, Ladan thought in alarm.

"No," Talia responded without realizing that he hadn't spoken the thought. "I am not being poisoned."

"Then, what?"

"I do not know." Secretly, Talia despaired the cause of her illness was the tension between her and Ladan that had risen over the past four weeks since the failed murder attempt. She thought once the threat of Menoth's revenge had been removed things would ease between her and Ladan. She had been wrong. Instead, the opposite had occurred and the tension had increased.

Joakim stopped by daily to see her and usually ended up telling her some story of how her mother or her sisters served the Alliance. Many of the ambassadors visited her or asked her to their homes, then would request her opinion on some thorny problem they faced, making her feel woefully inadequate. As far as she was concerned, they were according her a position of honor and respect that she had neither earned nor deserved.

In addition to all that, she was never without an Alcoran at her side. If she was not at the official residence, Noan or Seath were with her. Talia enjoyed her time with them, learning more of their natural temperament, but their presence drove a wedge between her and Ladan, one she was helpless to stop.

It bothered Talia that these people, who were eager to greet and talk with her, were reserved with Ladan, speaking to him only when necessary. More than once, Ladan had spent an entire evening sitting by himself in a corner of the room, drinking Mythinan brandy or Quintan wine.

The more she was drawn into the life of Ezion Geber and the affairs of the Alliance, the more distance there was between her and Ladan. He cut himself off from her, putting up mental barriers that prevented her from reading his mind. It seemed as if he were purposely pushing her away, when she needed more than ever to draw close to him. This new life frightened her, and the dizzy spells and queasiness of her stomach did nothing to ease her mind.

Ladan's voice intruded into her thoughts. "Get dressed. You're going to see a physician."

An hour later, she faced the doctor across his desk. "What is wrong with me?"

The man's pleased grin alerted Talia. "You're pregnant."

Totally unprepared for the announcement, her mouth dropped open.

"I see I've taken you by surprise."

"An understatement, sir."

"Well, knowing your history, it's not surprising that you are unaware of certain facts."

Her back stiffened. "I am not ignorant of biology. I know how species are propagated."

The doctor waved his hand in a dismissing gesture. "No, that's not what I meant. I was referring to bodily signs, such as soreness in your breasts, missing your woman's time, nausea, and dizziness."

Talia's face went scarlet and her eyes dropped to her lap. She heard the doctor rise and walk around his desk. She jerked back when he laid his hand on her shoulder.

"Talia, it's not my intent to embarrass you by talking about such intimate details that your mother or a close family female would tell you, but there is no one else. You will need to know certain facts to be prepared for the vast changes your body will sustain." The doctor scratched his chin. "Although with your mixed heritage, even I will have to guess at some things."

Her brow wrinkled with a frown. "What do you mean?"

"Geala physiology and Alcoran physiology, although similar, do differ slightly. Months of gestation, for instance, in the Geala is 11, in the Alcoran 10. And then we have to take into account Ladan's ancestry. You could have your child anywhere from 9 to 12 months. I cannot say. What is Ladan's heritage? If I know that, I can make a more educated guess."

A child. Hers and Ladan's. The idea was a balm to her troubled spirit.

"Talia?"

She shook her head, dispelling the dreams. "I must ask his permission before I can tell you his forbearers, but I am sure he will cooperate."

"Do you wish me to inform him?"

A radiant smile curved her lips. "No. I will give him the pleasing news myself."

When Talia walked into the waiting room, Noan was sitting with Ladan. Both men stood the moment they saw her.

"What did the doctor say?" Ladan asked.

Talia heard the concern in his voice and saw it in his golden eyes. She wanted to blurt out her glorious news, but Noan's presence restrained her. She would wait until they were alone. "I am well. Nothing is abnormal." The carefully worded answer was the exact truth.

"I'm glad," Noan interjected. "When I saw you and Ladan enter the doctor's office, I feared you were ill. Will you be able to attend Grandfather's dinner tonight?"

Talia wanted to stay home with Ladan this evening but knew Aram had planned this dinner with her in mind.

"She'll be there," Ladan said before she could respond. He clamped his hand around her wrist and walked away, leaving Noan to stare open-mouthed at the retreating couple.

Talia softly chastised him once they were home. "That was unnecessary, Ladan."

"You're wrong, Talia. It was entirely necessary,

because if I stood there one more second and watched that young pup drool over you, I would have broken him into a dozen little pieces."

Hope flared in Talia's heart. Ladan was jealous, which meant he cared. It was the first positive sign she had seen from him in a long time.

Talia reached out to him, but he stepped back, out of her reach. Her hand dropped to her side.

Ladan's face became an emotionless mask. "Be ready at 20.00 hours. I'll be back for you then."

The door slammed shut, shaking the house. Talia leaned against the wall. Why would he not allow her to touch him? She walked to the couch and sank down. She needed Ladan. Needed to touch him, be with him. Why was he acting so strange and distant?

She laughed aloud. The sound echoed in the empty room. How she had changed since she had first met him. She enjoyed the physical contact between herself and Ladan, felt no guilt at giving in to the urge to touch him in the privacy of their home. She laughed and smiled often, without feeling her emotions were out of control. She no longer feared her unknown half. The new feelings were bewildering, but not overwhelming.

And now she was with child—Ladan's child. A child to whom he could open his heart and give all the love he'd been denied.

Tears ran down her cheeks. *Oh, Ladan, my love, come back to me. I need you more than ever.*

Ladan arrived moments before his own deadline. His eyes drank in the sight of Talia dressed in the traditional Geala clothing. Her choice surprised him. He thought she would have worn the traditional Alcoran dress Aram had given her. He reached inside his vest and pulled what looked like Talia's gold circlet, but instead of the a plain gold band, a large blue stone was set in the vee.

"I want you to wear this," Ladan said, handing her the circlet. He still had the original one she had worn. He couldn't bear to part with it, so he had the jeweler copy it. He was letting her go. His brand would no longer hang on her forehead. "This is more appropriate for a princess."

Talia looked up in confusion. "Ladan?"

"I need to bathe and dress."

When he returned, Talia had removed the medallion and replaced it with the circlet. Ladan swallowed hard. She was every inch royalty. He took her arm and guided her outside to the TC. The trip to the reception passed in silence without a word or thought exchanged.

The feast Aram had prepared was lavish. Talia found that she enjoyed Alcoran food. The exquisite taste and wonderful texture of the dishes settled Talia's roiling stomach. Ladan sat silently by her side at the table, his black scowl discouraging anyone from talking to him. Talia flushed with embarrassment at his rude behavior.

After dinner, Ladan's conduct did not improve. As she watched, he grabbed a flagon of wine and disappeared. The polite conversation she engaged in taxed her, and she quickly retreated to the terrace outside the main room, where the guests were milling.

"Wait, Talia," Noan called. "I'll keep you company."

Inwardly, she groaned. She wished no company. Her thoughts were enough.

Noan's eyes roamed her face, lit by the golden glow of the moon. "You are very beautiful, Talia. Did you know that? As the dew on the rose poppy, you are that fresh and lovely."

She grew uneasy with his compliment. "Thank you."

"You are the talk of this city. All are impressed with your intelligence, wit and charm. Your place is among us. But . . ."

Talia tensed. "Finish what you have to say, Noan."

"It's just a shame you are burdened with that bounty hunter. If you were single, you would have your choice of any male—princes, leaders, wealthy men—who would gladly take you as wife."

A burning rage, such as she had never experienced in her life, sprung to life in Talia. For some strange and obscure reason, she wanted to hear the rest of Noan's planned speech. "I already have a husband."

"Divorce is legal throughout the Alliance."

Hidden among the trees in the garden, Ladan heard the entire exchange between Talia and Noan. When Noan mentioned divorce, something inside Ladan snapped. He didn't wait to hear Talia's response. He couldn't. Like a streaking comet, he ran out of the garden, around the large residence into the street. He did not worry about Talia's safety, for he knew Jeiel was at the party and would escort her home.

He had no idea where he was going, until he stopped before Ola's place of business. He entered the noisy, dimly-lit room. Several females were laughing and talking with the customers, and in a dark corner Ladan spotted Ola. As he approached her, the man she was with glanced up and froze. Ola looked in the direction of his stare.

"Why, Ladan, what a pleasant surprise. What brings you here?"

Ladan did not want to play the catty little game Ola was sure to initiate, so he pulled her to her feet and hauled her up to her room. Without a word of explanation, he lifted her and threw her down on the bed, following her down. His lips covered hers in an angry, punishing kiss. Instead of fighting the brutal assault, she responded to it, her hands clutching Ladan's back.

Something was wrong. He felt nothing. No excitement, no thrill. He sat up and took a deep breath. Ola scrambled to her knees and hugged him from behind. He pushed away the encircling arms and stood.

"What is it, Ladan?"

He looked down at her puzzled expression. If the situation wasn't so pathetic, he'd laugh. He'd been hurting and burning with anger when he had left Talia, and the idea of lashing out against the Geala bond of fidelity appealed to him. But the taste of Ola's lips on his, the feel of her body under his, left him cold. She didn't taste of innocence and honey. She didn't smell fresh like the first breeze of Spring. She wasn't Talia.

He laughed bitterly. Finally, his Geala heritage caught hold, strangling him with its strength.

"It's your wife, isn't it Ladan? Has she so emasculated you that you cannot lie with another woman?"

Ladan's face hardened and Ola scooted back on the bed.

"No, Ola, she has not unmanned me. She has just taught me how much better wine is from a single cup than many. She also taught me the value of discrimination."

As he walked away, Ola's scream of outrage told him his words had hit their mark. He grinned.

Talia felt the curious urge to strike Noan right between his lovely blue eyes. Too late had she realized that Ladan was nearby. Although she did not hear or see him leave the garden, she felt it in the deepest part of her soul. She only hoped she could find him later and repair the damage Noan's rampant mouth had done.

"Divorce?" she carefully said.

A flash of doubt crossed Noan's face. "Yes."

She took a deep breath, trying to gain control of herself. She would not respond in anger. "I am afraid you and everyone in the Alliance have underestimated my Geala half. Although I do not resemble my father, I was raised on his teachings. The bond between Ladan and myself is unbreakable. It would be easier to cut off my right arm than to divorce him. How can one divide one's soul? How could I leave the father of my child?"

"Child?" Noan squeaked.

"Oh, yes, Noan. I am with child. I doubt many of those high-level men you mentioned would desire a woman large with child—a child not of their own flesh."

"But how can you love so brutal a man when you are so gentle? Do you know his reputation? What he has done? How many men he's killed? How easily he does it?"

"Stop. Do not continue. Yes, I know. Ladan told me himself of his reputation. He warned me. But he has also guarded me with his life against great odds, thoughtfully cared for me, and brought me safely here. He may be all those things to others, but to me he is husband." She turned and walked into the building.

"Wait, Talia." Noan ran to catch up with her. "Will you stay here, or go back to Petar?"

"I cannot say. I only know I must find Ladan."

* * *

Talia quickly said her good-byes to Aram and the other dignitaries, then sought out Jeiel. She knew Ladan would wish her to have an escort, so she sought out the bounty hunter. She found him talking to a beautiful young woman.

"Forgive the interruption," she said, feeling awkward breaking into the intimate scene, "but may I speak with you, Jeiel?"

He whispered in the woman's ear, then kissed her forehead. Talia tried not to look.

"What may I do for you?" Jeiel asked.

"Ladan has left the reception without me. I need an escort home."

"Oh?" The tone of his voice made her squirm. "How do you know he departed and is not just in some corner getting drunk?"

The pain in her eyes told the story. He asked no further questions but gestured towards the front door.

As they walked swiftly toward the TC, Jeiel asked, "Do you want to tell me about it?"

"Ladan overhead Noan ask me why I did not divorce him and marry someone more worthy."

Jeiel whistled. "I'm surprised Ladan didn't break the youth in half."

"I became aware of his presence too late. He left before he could hear my response to Noan's question."

"Which was?" Jeiel asked as he pressed the summons button for the TC.

Talia recounted what she had said, then added, "You should have seen his comical expression when I told him I was with child."

"Whoa! Back up. You're pregnant?"

She nodded.

"Have you told Ladan?"

The door to the TC opened. She waited until they were moving before answering. "No. I have tried to tell him all day but have not had an opportunity."

"Really?"

"I do not understand what has come over him. He has erected barriers in his mind and heart, not allowing me to cross them. When we returned from the doctor this morning, he dropped me off at the house, then vanished until moments before we were to leave for Aram's dinner. What is wrong, Jeiel? Why is he pushing me away?"

"I'm afraid, Talia, Ladan feels the same as Noan, that you deserve someone better."

"But that is not how I feel. These people want my mother, not me. I cannot be what I am not."

"What is it you want?"

"What I would like is to go back to my high valley on Petar with Ladan and have this child. But I know that is not possible. I have responsibilities, to Ladan, to the Alliance. I will work for the Alliance, but only as Ladan's mate."

"I'm glad to hear that."

"Now, if I can only convince him of that."

Jeiel walked slowly toward the TC. He marveled that the strength of emotion that existed between Ladan and Talia. Love, romantics would call it. He didn't believe such an emotion existed. Yet he was hard pressed to give a name to the thing that existed between Ladan and Talia. Whatever that thing was, he envied them. To bad such a lucky accident would never happened to him.

Ladan climbed one of the high hills on the west side of the city and settled himself among the boulders. He gazed down at the glittering lights for a long time. He'd been a fool. He loved Talia, but he could not let her go. It didn't matter that he was not good enough. He needed her and could not envision the rest of his life without her. Tonight certainly proved that. It had never occurred to him that he would not desire another woman. Except Talia.

She was his, and he'd be damned if he'd step aside and let some pasty-face youth take his place.

He shook his head. So much for his noble gesture of love, but then again, he wasn't known for his good deeds.

He stood. It was time he set things right.

Talia was unbraiding her hair when the doorbell chimed. Her stomach knotted with unease.

"Who is there?" she called, peeking through the clear side panel by the door.

A man stepped from the shadows into the light of the streetlamp. She recognized Artis, Joakim's secretary, a moment before he said his name. "May I come in? It's very hard to talk through this door."

She hesitated.

"Ladan has had an accident. I've been sent to bring you to him."

He was lying. Ladan would not send this stranger for her. "I will call Joakim and confirm your story."

Just as she stepped back from the door, the lock exploded, and Artis rushed in, a laser in his hand.

"Ah, I see your telepathic ability wasn't exaggerated," he said.

"You are the traitor," Talia whispered, horrified.

"Right again," he answered. "You're amazing. So amazing, in fact, that I probably don't need to tell you how I went to General Milon's home after learning of Gretis' death, and killed him, giving Ladan his traitor. Do I?"

"My telepathic abilities are limited."

"Really, or are you just trying to keep me off guard? Well, just in case you can't read my mind, I'll tell you what I want you to do. Step outside and go to the TC. And don't make a sound, or I'll shoot you. You and I are going to take a little trip to see Menoth."

"He was killed in the final battle between the Alliance and Union."

"No, he is alive and well, and waiting to meet you."

Fear shot through Talia's heart.

Artis motioned with his gun for Talia to move.

"Ladan will know what has happened to me and follow," she said over her shoulder as she walked out of the house.

"That's what we're counting on." They stopped before the TC. When the door slid open, Artis checked the unit to make sure it was empty, then shoved Talia inside. After punching in his destination, he sat beside her, the laser pointed at her side.

"Why are you doing this?" Talia asked as the car raced through the tunnels.

"Ladan understands. I finally got tired of always being so close to power, but never really having any. I thought the Alliance would lose. Menoth offered me the position as the head administrator of the Union if I succeeded in this mission. How could I refuse?"

"What of loyalty and honor?"

"They come in a poor second to power and wealth."

"Does Menoth have anything left to give you now?"

Artis's hand whipped out and caught her cheek. "I value my life. If I hadn't brought you to him, my life would have been forfeited. I didn't have to think twice about the choice."

The unit stopped, and Artis pushed Talia toward one of the private ships parked in the landing bay.

Ladan, she silently cried when she noticed how deserted the area was. She spotted Jeiel's ship and surged forward, trying to break Artis's hold on her arm. He jerked her back.

"Don't do anything foolish," he hissed in her ear.

"What's going on here?" At the sound of Jeiel's voice, Talia's heart raced.

Jeiel moved toward the couple, his head cocked as he studied them. "Talia, what are you doing down here?"

Before she could answer, Artis raised the laser and fired, creasing the side of Jeiel's skull with the beam. He fell at Talia's feet.

"No!" she screamed, dropping to her knees.

"Come on," Artis growled, pulling her to her feet.

She fought him as he dragged her across the bay to his ship. Artis shoved her through the door, then turned to close it. Talia's fist landed behind his ear, causing him to howl in pain.

"That's enough." He tackled her, sending them to the floor. Artis grabbed two handfuls of hair and banged her head against the floor until she lost consciousness.

HUNTER'S HEART

* * *

Ladan stopped in the middle of the street. His heart jerked in response to Talia's cry for help. She was in trouble. He didn't bother going home or back to the party at Aram's house. His gut told him Menoth had somehow had snatched Talia.

He raced for the nearest TC. Once at the landing bay, Ladan went to the controller's office.

"Has any ship taken off in the last hour?" he asked the startled man.

"Only one. MVE400-34."

"To whom is it registered?"

The clerk punched up the information on the screen before him. "Officially, the vessel belongs to Joakim."

"Was he the pilot?"

"I cannot say, sir. The individual did not identify himself."

"And you just allow anyone to fly off with Joakim's personal ship?"

At Ladan's harsh tone, the young man jumped to his feet and backed up a step. "Uh—he knew the release code for the vessel."

"Wonderful. That narrows the choice to a few dozen people. Call Joakim, you fool. See if he is in the city."

"By what authority are you giving these orders?" asked a senior officer, stepping into the room.

Ladan whirled, grabbed the man around the throat with one hand and pinned him against the wall. The officer's eyes rolled back in his head as he clutched Ladan's arm. Ladan ignored the man's efforts. "Call Joakim," he commanded the other man.

The moment Ladan heard Joakim's voice, he released

the officer. Ladan looked pointedly at the officer's laser. "Don't try it. You'll be dead before your weapon clears its holster," he warned. He moved confidently to the view screen to talk to Joakim.

"Did you authorize anyone to take your private ship?"

"No."

"Who knows the release code for the ship?"

"About seven or eight individuals."

"Does Artis know the code?"

Joakim paused. "Yes, but why do you ask?"

Ladan cursed. Violently. Everyone in the room jumped at the harsh sound. "It makes sense. Why didn't I see it sooner? Artis is the traitor, not General Milon. Artis killed Milon to throw suspicion off himself, allowing him time to finished his plan. He's taken Talia to Menoth."

"What?" Joakim cried.

The door to the office opened and Jeiel stumbled in. "Ladan, Artis took Talia. I tried to stop him, but—"

Ladan laid his hand on Jeiel's shoulder. "I know. What I need now is your ship."

"It's yours."

"Thanks." He looked at the screen and spoke to Joakim. "Have your fighters follow."

"Certainly."

Ladan turned to Jeiel. "If I don't return, everything I own is yours."

Jeiel smiled. "You'll return, because I'll be right behind you guarding your rear."

Chapter 17

When Talia woke, she found her wrists tied to the co-pilot's chair. Her head ached abominably. It was becoming a nasty habit, being hit on the head.

"I see you are finally awake."

Talia turned her head and looked at Artis. The movement made her stomach roll, and her face lost all color.

"Are you not feeling well, my dear? Well, you'll feel even worse once I hand you over to Menoth, I assure you."

Talia shuddered. Hell was before her. She just prayed that she could conduct herself with dignity.

She said nothing for the next few hours. Instead, she tried to bolster her courage by focusing on Ladan. Artis's voice, transmitting a message, broke into her thoughts.

"Is the female with you?" a disembodied voice asked.

"Yes, I have her."

"Land. Someone will be waiting for you."

The radio fell silent.

Talia looked out window and saw a large asteroid. "This is not Darka," Talia said.

"You're most observant. The trip to Darka would have taken too long. Menoth was eager to meet you, so we decided this asteroid would be perfect."

"But why here?"

"Why don't you ask Menoth? I'm sure he can satisfy any curiosity you have."

From Artis's tone, Talia knew that he was not referring to head knowledge about the asteroid.

Too quickly they were on the ground, and Artis cut the engines. He opened the hatch, then untied her. When she stood, two Dyne soldiers stood within the door of the ship. They said nothing, but marched to her side, grasped her arms, and escorted her out into a small covered landing bay. Moving down a short hall, past a set of double doors, they arrived in an empty room. They left her in the center of the chamber, retreating to stand by the door.

Artis paced around the edge of the room. When the automatic doors opened, he jumped and scurried behind Talia. The man standing in the doorway was tall, with broad shoulders and trim waist. His silver hair hung past his shoulders, and a jagged scar ran from his left eye to the corner of his nose. The scaling across the back of his hands and forehead was more pronounced than any Dyne she'd seen before. His green eyes glowed with an unnatural fire that made him resemble some evil being from the darkest part of the galaxy. Menoth.

He walked toward her. Malevolence, like a magnetic field, surrounded him. He circled her, studying her from head to toe. He picked up a strand of gold hair that hung wildly around her shoulders. As he rubbed a silken curl, he stared at the tattoo on her forehead. Suddenly, he reached out and seized her hand.

Revulsion welled up in Talia, but she did not try to yank her hand away from Menoth as he pulled back the fingers of her left hand.

"So, you are a Geala. At least part of you. You're a half-blood, just like Ladan." He did not release her. Instead, with his free hand he caressed her face. "Your skin is soft and golden." His fingers ran down her neck, then grasped her chin, forcing her eyes to his. "You'll pay in blood for making me lose to the Alliance. After I've killed Ladan, I'll make you wish for death a thousand times a day."

Talia raised her chin a notch.

"You don't believe me?" Menoth asked. Before she could respond, he pinched the muscle at the base of her neck between his thumb and forefinger. Agonizing pain shot up into her head and down her arm. He applied more pressed until she moaned and fell to her knees.

"Let that be a lesson to you," he said, shoving her away. Talia sprawled onto the floor. Menoth addressed the guards. "Take her into the prepared chamber and put a slave collar on her."

When Talia had left, Menoth turned to Artis. "I'm surprised you were able to pull off this kidnaping. You've not done much else right."

"Ladan is a formidable foe."

"And you're a blundering idiot."

"There were a few mistakes, I'll admit."

"A few!" Menoth thundered. "Because of you I've lost my empire."

"I gave you the correct information about Ladan's

location. I cannot be held responsible for others's incompetence."

"Are you calling me incompetent?" Menoth's words had the chill of death.

Artis backed up. "No, Menoth, no. I meant nothing of the kind."

The door slid open and a guard entered. "Sir, a vessel has been picked up by the computer."

"Ladan?"

"We believe so."

"Good. Leave the shields down. No one is to challenge him. Bring him to me when he lands. Understand?"

"Yes, sir."

Menoth turned to Artis. "It seems your usefulness is at an end." He backed the younger man into a corner and clamped his hands around Artis's throat.

"I've always found it much more satisfying to kill my victims with my bare hands than with any weapon. That way you can feel their struggles, smell their fear, hear their pleas and gasps for breath."

His hands tightened, cutting off Artis's breath. "You failed me, Artis, and for that you must pay with your life."

Artis's fingers clawed Menoth's hands, but the Dyne's strength was far greater than his. His eyes bugged out and his face turned red. Impatient with the dying man, Menoth placed his thumbs at the base of Artis' throat and punched his digits through Artis's larynx. Death was instantaneous. Menoth threw the body aside. He didn't look back as he left the room. The guard would take care of the trash.

* * *

With the tracking devices of the Alliance, Ladan followed Artis to the asteroid 40-MQ-678, in the alpha section of the star system between fourth and fifth planets of star 40-MQ.

As he flew by the planet Ditan, Ladan recalled his father talking about the retreat he had built for himself in case he lost his power and could not go back to Darka. He didn't know where that retreat was until now. It made sense for Menoth to come to this asteroid. Darka was on the far side of the star system, clustered with all the other members of the Dyne Union, a good eight star days's travel, and the first place the Alliance forces would look. Here, on 40-MQ-678, Menoth could hide right in their midst.

"Welcome, Ladan," a voice crackled over the open channel of ship's transmitter.

Menoth. Ladan froze when he heard the voice.

"I'm waiting for you."

Ladan said nothing, but piloted his vessel down to the asteroid. He checked his weapons, knives and laser, then popped the hatch. A single soldier stood by the door leading away from the landing bay.

"This way," he said, turned, and walked down the hall.

Ladan harnessed the hate thundering through his veins and followed the soldier. The corridor twisted and turned until they came to a closed door. The man pressed a button on the wall and the door opened. He motioned for Ladan to precede him.

Every muscle in Ladan's body went taut as he entered

the room. He ignored the dozen soldiers milling about. Instead, his eyes locked with Menoth's.

Like a caged beast clawing at the walls of its prison, Ladan's hate wreathed, nearly shattering his control. Visions of his mother's broken and bleeding body rose up before his eyes.

Talia. He was here to rescue her, and losing control would not accomplish that. Ladan pulled off his armband and threw it at Menoth's feet. "I challenge you to a Ketea." Ladan knew Menoth would be unable to refuse the traditional Dyne challenge to fight to the death in front of all these soldiers. It was his only chance of getting Talia and himself out of this place alive.

Bending down, Menoth retrieved the band. He slipped the thick bracelet from his wrist and pitched it at Ladan. "I accept." He looked at the officer next to him. "Go prepare the room." Crossing his arms, he studied Ladan. "You've grown."

"I'm not interested in exchanging pleasantries with you. I want to see Talia."

"You aren't in a position to threaten, boy, so watch your tongue."

Ladan's lips tightened, and a muscle in his jaw hardened, but he remained silent.

Menoth smiled. "That's better. I've followed your career from afar these past few years, and have been impressed with the ruthless reputation you've gained. I thought to myself that I'm responsible for your success."

"Oh, yes, you're the reason I'm the twisted, vengeful man I am today. In fact, when we fight the Ketea, you'll see what a good teacher you were."

A surge of satisfaction shot through Ladan as he watched doubt darken Menoth's face. "I want to see Talia."

"A reasonable request. I will give you two uninterrupted star hours with her. It's the least I can do for a dying man."

When the door to Talia's room opened and Ladan noticed the slave collar around her neck, he grasped the soldier by the front of his uniform. "Why is she wearing that collar?"

"Menoth ordered it," the quaking solder responded.

Ladan threw the man into the hall, then punched the CLOSE button on the door. He crossed the room in three strides and pulled Talia into his arms. A small whimper escaped her throat.

"My tenata," he crooned, soothingly. "All will be well."

Pushing away from his comforting arms, she looked up. "How?"

A scowl crossed Ladan's face as he stared at the heavy metal tube that encircled Talia's delicate neck. He'd like to break the collar with his hands, but he knew that if the collar was removed by any other means than the special key that deactivated the current running through the metal, Talia would receive enough electricity to kill her.

"I have challenged Menoth to a Ketea, a duel."

"And he accepted?"

"He would have lost face if he had refused. On Darka, a Ketea is almost a sacred event. No man with any pride would refuse." He scanned her face. "Are you all right? Did Artis hurt you in any way?"

She shook her head. "I am sorry—"

"No." Ladan laid a finger across her lips, stopping her apology. "I'm the one at fault. If I hadn't left you, none of this would've happened."

"You are not to blame. I think Artis would have found another time, another place."

"Perhaps."

The air was charged with the things they wanted to say to one another. Neither knew how to begin.

"You left the garden too soon, Ladan," Talia said, breaking the heavy silence.

"You knew I was there?" He sounded perplexed.

"Too late I sensed you were there. I was too upset by what Noan said. You did not hear my response to him."

"What did you say?"

"I told him that I could never divorce you. You are my other half, Ladan. The completing part of my heart and soul. I would die without you."

He wrapped his arms around her waist and buried his face in her hair.

"Besides," she sweetly whispered, "how could I leave the father of my child?"

His head snapped up. "What?"

"I am with child."

"When did you find out?"

Her eyes dropped to his chest. "When you took me to the doctor. He told me then."

"Why didn't you not tell me sooner?"

"Because you never gave me the opportunity. The minute we returned from the doctor, you were off again."

Guilt punched him in the gut. She was right. He hadn't given her time to tell him. The idea of his babe growing in Talia's body sent a warmth flowing through him. Now, it was even more important to defeat Menoth. Three lives depended on his victory.

He threaded his fingers through her hair, cupping the back of her head. "Sweet moon child," he breathed, lowering his head. His lips brushed over hers, causing her to sigh with pleasure. Encouraged by her reaction, he deepened the kiss, tasting again the honey of her mouth. He drew back, breathing heavily.

"Ah, Talia, I've been a fool. I felt because you were a princess you deserved a mate of higher status than me, but I didn't count on the Geala bond that holds me as firmly as it held you. Fidelity is a strange concept, but one I've become familiar with. I desire no other than you."

"I love you, Ladan."

"I don't know what love is, Talia, so I cannot vow my love to you. But I do know that I want you with me. Always. I cannot conceive of life without you."

She touched his cheek. "Do not worry. There is a tenderness within your heart that will grow as it is nurtured."

"And will you nurture it?"

"Every moment for the rest of my life."

The door to the room opened and a guard entered, carrying a folded white garment. "When you are ready, I will escort you to the battle chamber." He whirled and left.

Calmly, Ladan began to strip. First he removed the belts crossing his chest, then vest, and boots. When he started to unfasten his pants, Talia asked, "What are you doing?"

"Preparing for the Ketea." He slid his pants down his legs.

"Are you going to fight like that?" she choked, eyes wide.

"In ancient time, when the Ketea was fought, the combatants were nude. As civilization intruded upon us, we bowed to outsiders' shock and dressed in loincloths." As he talked, he slipped the white cloth under the thong tied around his hips.

Kneeling, he withdrew his knives from their sheaths and gave Talia one. "Hide this on your body. If I don't win or the Alliance forces don't arrive, use it."

"On whom?"

"If you think you can kill Menoth with a single blow, then use it on him. If not . . . I would not see you suffer as my mother did."

Her hand shook as she took the anlace and slid it under her coat-dress into the waistband of her pants.

Ladan stood. "Come. It's time to go." He held out his hand to her.

The guard led them down the hall to the last door. All the individuals on the asteroid were gathered in the large room. A blast of heat roared out of the room as they entered, catching Talia by surprise.

In the center of the room was a deep pit, glowing with the dancing flames burning in its belly. Suspended over the mouth of the pit by thick metal braces was a thin platform. Smaller than the circumference of the pit, the platform left a meter's distance between its edge and the lip of the hole. Two gangways led from the floor of the chamber to the platform.

Talia grew sick at the sight before her. She knew that platform, no matter what it was made of, would scorch the bare feet of both men. She looked from Ladan to Menoth, who had been there when they entered, and knew this fight was to the death. She shuddered.

Oh, my love, she thought. *Be careful.*

Ladan turned to her. *I will.*

An officer, who was to act as referee, motioned the combatants forward, then handed each man a spiked, metal ball with a long-handle. In addition to that, each man held a knife.

Next, the referee moved toward Talia. This time, in each hand, he held a piece of jewelry—Ladan's armband and Menoth's bracelet. He raised the pieces over his head, then set them down at her feet.

"The victor will own the female. If the challenger, Ladan, wins, he and the female will go free."

A large metal gong sounded, and both men walked to different gangways. When the gong was hit a second time, they crossed to the platform. The battle had begun.

Talia gasped when she telepathically felt the heat scorch the skin off the bottom of Ladan's feet.

Ladan ignored the burning pain shooting up his legs and ignored Talia's choked gasp. Instead, he concentrated on the fight before him. Talia was all he had. All that would ever matter to him. She had reached deep inside his soul, past the barriers and scars of hate and viciousness, to touch the kernel of softness left in him. He could not lose her now.

Ladan circled Menoth, taking the measure of his enemy. Menoth struck first, swinging the metal ball in a wide arc. Ladan jumped back, his heels going over the edge of the platform. As he struggled to regain his balance, Menoth's blade cut across his forearm.

Talia bit back the moan she felt as the blade cut Ladan's flesh. His pain swamped her and she did not know how he continued the battle.

"I'm disappointed, Ladan," Menoth taunted. "You're not much of a fighter."

Ladan's response was to swing his weapon at a sharp upward arch, catching Menoth's shoulder. The sound of heavy metal tearing the skin and bone made Talia gag. Menoth roared in pain and charged.

Unable to endure the sight, Talia closed her eyes, but she could not stop her ears or blot out her sensations. Each time Ladan was hit, she experienced his suffering.

Time seemed endless, stuck in this one horrible instant of time, refusing to move forward. Finally, she heard the swish of the metal ball, followed by a piercing scream. Her eyes snapped open. Ladan stood at the edge of the platform, looking down into the burning interior. He felt Talia's eyes upon him and raised his head. Blood and sweat coated his body, but in his eyes Talia found the reassurance she needed.

He limped over the gangway to where she stood. He picked up his armband, then took Talia's hand. He paused and scanned the room.

"Does anyone dispute my right to leave with this woman?" Ladan challenged.

None answered.

Ladan turned to the nearest soldier. "Unlock her slave collar."

The man scurried forward and offered Ladan the key.

He shook his head. "No, you do it."

The man's hands shook as he inserted the key and turned the lock. The collar sprung open. The soldier stepped back, allowing Ladan the honor of removing the collar. With great care, Ladan freed Talia.

He looked around the room. He didn't worry about these soldiers. The Alliance forces would soon arrive and take care of them.

With a curt nod of his head, he walked with Talia out of the room.

"Ladan, we must get you medical help."

"I'm fine, Talia."

Her eyes welled with tears. "You have endured so much."

He slid his arm around her shoulders and drew her close. Everything that was dear to him was safe. For once the future looked bright. "I won and everything else is insignificant."

He was right.

Chapter 18

Ladan watched as his very pregnant wife walked among the new shoots in the garden she had recently planted. He scanned the valley, sown with grains and vegetables. This was a good place to raise children. As he lay in bed recuperating from his wounds, he had decided that he could not take Talia from her duties to the Alliance, yet he knew she longed for her quiet mountain valley. When he was well, he combed Gemmal, looking for a special place for Talia. He had found it a day's walk from Ezion Geber. Before he brought her to the valley, he had built a home for her similar to the one she had on Petar. Talia had instantly loved the valley and cried when she first saw it.

He grinned broadly when he saw her bend to inspect a single bud. He smiled much more often now. Talia filled his days and nights. The anger that had driven him before was gone. He was at peace with himself. Talia had been the peacemaker.

He heard Talia singing softly to herself as she wandered about her garden. She was different, too. Although he knew her ways would always be formal, she had stopped battling her Alcoran half and was easy with her new-found freedom to laugh and cry, to touch and kiss. He was glad Joakim had offered him the job of security chief for the Alliance. That way, he was here to enjoy Talia's new-found freedom.

Silently, he crept up behind her, but he knew she sensed his presence long before his arm encircled her waist, or what was left of it.

"How are you feeling?" Ladan nuzzled her ear.

"Like a very fat, ungainly female."

"No, you are just being fruitful, like your garden." His hand slid down to cover her abdomen.

She swatted his hand. "There are times when I think I will never have this child," she grumbled. "That I was born pregnant."

"It will soon end."

"When, Ladan? It's been ten-and-a-half months."

"You know what the doctor said. It could come any day."

"Or be six more weeks."

Grasping her shoulders, he turned her to face him. "I wish there was something I could do to help."

She raised her eyebrow. "You have done quite enough."

Ladan threw back his head and laughed. The sound was sweet music to her ears.

Suddenly, a squeezing pain gripped her middle.

"Talia." Ladan's eyes brimmed with concern.

When she could catch her breath, she smiled at him. "Summon the doctor. It's time."

Ladan sat with Talia through her hours of labor.

Although the doctor objected and Talia thought it inappropriate, he refused to leave her side. As the pains increased, Talia was glad Ladan was there to give encouragement and share the experience. Thirty hours after the onset of labor, Talia gave birth to a daughter.

Ladan took the child from the doctor and carefully cleaned the small, wailing creature.

After wrapping the child in a blanket, he gave her to Talia.

"Are you pleased?" Talia asked, anxious that Ladan might be disappointed the child was a girl.

His smile was radiant. "She is beautiful. Thank you, *my tenata.*"

Ladan sat in the silvery glow of the moonlight, his daughter cradled in his arms. He examined each limb, fingers and toes, noting that her skin was smooth everywhere on her tiny body. Her hair was black, her eyes blue, and in her left palm a blue star. She was beautiful. Perfect. Along with her mother, they were gift from heaven for a man who had lived in hell.

"Ladan," Talia's soft voice called.

"I'm coming, little Geala. I'm coming."

He smiled down at his daughter. "Let's go, my lady. Your mother is waiting."

The child smiled back at him.

His heart swelled with love.

ROMANCE FROM JO BEVERLY

DANGEROUS JOY   (0-8217-5129-8, $5.99)

FORBIDDEN   (0-8217-4488-7, $4.99)

THE SHATTERED ROSE   (0-8217-5310-X, $5.99)

TEMPTING FORTUNE   (0-8217-4858-0, $4.99)

Available wherever paperbacks are sold, or order direct from the Publisher. Send cover price plus 50¢ per copy for mailing and handling to Penguin USA, P.O. Box 999, c/o Dept. 17109, Bergenfield, NJ 07621. Residents of New York and Tennessee must include sales tax. DO NOT SEND CASH.

WATCH FOR THESE REGENCY ROMANCES

BREACH OF HONOR   (0-8217-5111-5, $4.50)
by Phylis Warady

DeLACEY'S ANGEL   (0-8217-4978-1, $3.99)
by Monique Ellis

A DECEPTIVE BEQUEST   (0-8217-5380-0, $4.50)
by Olivia Sumner

A RAKE'S FOLLY   (0-8217-5007-0, $3.99)
by Claudette Williams

AN INDEPENDENT LADY   (0-8217-3347-8, $3.95)
by Lois Stewart

Available wherever paperbacks are sold, or order direct from the Publisher. Send cover price plus 50¢ per copy for mailing and handling Penguin USA, P.O. Box 999, c/o Dept. 17109, Bergenfield, NJ 07621. Residents of New York and Tennessee must include sales tax. DO NOT SEND CASH.

LOOK FOR THESE REGENCY ROMANCES

SCANDAL'S DAUGHTER   (0-8217-5273-1, $4.50)
by Carola Dunn

A DANGEROUS AFFAIR   (0-8217-5294-4, $4.50)
by Mona Gedney

A SUMMER COURTSHIP   (0-8217-5358-4, $4.50)
by Valerie King

TIME'S TAPESTRY   (0-8217-5381-9, $4.99)
by Joan Overfield

LADY STEPHANIE   (0-8217-5341-X, $4.50)
by Jeanne Savery

Available wherever paperbacks are sold, or order direct from the Publisher. Send cover price plus 50¢ per copy for mailing and handling Penguin USA, P.O. Box 999, c/o Dept. 17109, Bergenfield, NJ 07621. Residents of New York and Tennessee must include sales tax. DO NOT SEND CASH.

WATCH FOR THESE ZEBRA REGENCIES

LADY STEPHANIE (0-8217-5341-X, $4.50)
by Jeanne Savery
Lady Stephanie Morris has only one true love: the family estate she has managed ever since her mother died. But then Lord Anthony Rider arrives on her estate, claiming he has plans for both the land and the woman. Stephanie soon realizes she's fallen in love with a man whose sensual caresses will plunge her into a world of peril and intrigue . . . a man as dangerous as he is irresistible.

BRIGHTON BEAUTY (0-8217-5340-1, $4.50)
by Marilyn Clay
Chelsea Grant, pretty and poor, naively takes school friend Alayna Marchmont's place and spends a month in the country. The devastating man had sailed from Honduras to claim his promised bride, Miss Marchmont. An affair of the heart may lead to disaster . . . unless a resourceful Brighton beauty finds a way to stop a masquerade and keep a lord's love.

LORD DIABLO'S DEMISE (0-8217-5338-X, $4.50)
by Meg-Lynn Roberts
The sinfully handsome Lord Harry Glendower was a gambler and the black sheep of his family. About to be forced into a marriage of convenience, the devilish fellow engineered his own demise, never having dreamed that faking his death would lead him to the heavenly refuge of spirited heiress Gwyn Morgan, the daughter of a physician.

A PERILOUS ATTRACTION (0-8217-5339-8, $4.50)
by Dawn Aldridge Poore
Alissa Morgan is stunned when a frantic passenger thrusts her baby into Alissa's arms and flees, having heard rumors that a notorious highwayman posed a threat to their coach. Handsome stranger Hugh Sebastian secretly possesses the treasured necklace the highwayman seeks and volunteers to pose as Alissa's husband to save her reputation. With a lost baby and missing necklace in their care, the couple embarks on a journey into peril—and passion.

Available wherever paperbacks are sold, or order direct from the Publisher. Send cover price plus 50¢ per copy for mailing and handling to Penguin USA, P.O. Box 999, c/o Dept. 17109, Bergenfield, NJ 07621. Residents of New York and Tennessee must include sales tax. DO NOT SEND CASH.